808.83
L52g

DOVER·THRIFT·EDITIONS

Green Tea and Other Ghost Stories

J. SHERIDAN LeFANU

TRINIDAD HIGH SCHOOL
LIBRARY

D0189986

DOVER PUBLICATIONS, INC.
New York

27,446

DOVER THRIFT EDITIONS

GENERAL EDITOR: STANLEY APPELBAUM
EDITOR OF THIS VOLUME: PHILIP SMITH

Copyright

Copyright © 1993 by Dover Publications, Inc.
All rights reserved under Pan American and International Copyright Conventions.

Published in Canada by General Publishing Company, Ltd., 30 Lesmill Road, Don Mills, Toronto, Ontario.
Published in the United Kingdom by Constable and Company, Ltd., 3 The Lanchesters, 162–164 Fulham Palace Road, London W6 9ER.

Bibliographical Note

This Dover edition, first published in 1993, is a new selection of ghost stories by J. Sheridan LeFanu, reprinted from standard texts (see Note, opposite, for sources). The selection was made and the introductory Note specially written for this edition by John Grafton.

Library of Congress Cataloging-in-Publication Data

Le Fanu, Joseph Sheridan, 1814–1873.
   Green tea and other ghost stories / J. Sheridan LeFanu.
      p.   cm. — (Dover thrift editions)
   ISBN 0-486-27795-X (pbk.)
   1. Ghost stories, English. I. Title. II. Series.
PR4879.L7A6   1993
823′.8—dc20   93-11037
                                             CIP

Manufactured in the United States of America
Dover Publications, Inc., 31 East 2nd Street, Mineola, N.Y. 11501

Note

JOSEPH SHERIDAN LEFANU was born in Dublin on August 28, 1814, and died there on February 7, 1873. A grandnephew of the dramatist Richard Brinsley Sheridan, LeFanu was educated at Dublin's Trinity College. He studied for the legal profession, but abandoned this career for journalism while still a young man. He was the editor and publisher of several Irish newspapers and periodicals including the *Dublin Evening Mail* and the *Dublin University Magazine*. A shy and somewhat reclusive personality, LeFanu was the prolific author of fourteen novels (of which *Uncle Silas*, *The House by the Churchyard* and *Wylder's Hand* are the most highly regarded today) and approximately thirty short stories of the supernatural, the fiction on which his reputation clearly rests over a century after his death. Among Victorian writers, he was unexcelled as a writer in the realm of supernatural terror. The present collection reprints four prime examples of his craftsmanship and artistry in this entertaining form. "Green Tea" is reprinted from the 1886 edition of a collection of LeFanu's fiction, *In a Glass Darkly*; "Squire Toby's Will" and "Sir Dominick's Bargain" are reprinted from the 1923 collection *Madam Crowl's Ghost, and Other Tales of Mystery*; and "The Fortunes of Sir Robert Ardagh" is reprinted from the *Dublin University Magazine*, 1838.

Contents

Green Tea

PROLOGUE

Martin Hesselius, the German Physician

Though carefully educated in medicine and surgery, I have never practised either. The study of each continues, nevertheless, to interest me profoundly. Neither idleness nor caprice caused my secession from the honourable calling which I had just entered. The cause was a very trifling scratch inflicted by a dissecting knife. This trifle cost me the loss of two fingers, amputated promptly, and the more painful loss of my health, for I have never been quite well since, and have seldom been twelve months together in the same place.

In my wanderings I became acquainted with Dr. Martin Hesselius, a wanderer like myself, like me a physician, and like me an enthusiast in his profession. Unlike me in this, that his wanderings were voluntary, and he a man, if not of fortune, as we estimate fortune in England, at least in what our forefathers used to term "easy circumstances." He was an old man when I first saw him; nearly five-and-thirty years my senior.

In Dr. Martin Hesselius, I found my master. His knowledge was immense, his grasp of a case was an intuition. He was the very man to inspire a young enthusiast, like me, with awe and delight. My admiration has stood the test of time and survived the separation of death. I am sure it was well-founded.

For nearly twenty years I acted as his medical secretary. His immense collection of papers he has left in my care, to be arranged, indexed and bound. His treatment of some of these cases is curious. He writes in two distinct characters. He describes what he saw and heard as an intelligent layman might, and when in this style of narrative he had seen the patient either through his own hall-door, to the light of day, or through the gates of darkness to

1

the caverns of the dead, he returns upon the narrative, and in the terms of his art and with all the force and originality of genius, proceeds to the work of analysis, diagnosis and illustration.

Here and there a case strikes me as of a kind to amuse or horrify a lay reader with an interest quite different from the peculiar one which it may possess for an expert. With slight modifications, chiefly of language, and of course a change of names, I copy the following. The narrator is Dr. Martin Hesselius. I find it among the voluminous notes of cases which he made during a tour in England about sixty-four years ago.

It is related in series of letters to his friend Professor Van Loo of Leyden. The professor was not a physician, but a chemist, and a man who read history and metaphysics and medicine, and had, in his day, written a play.

The narrative is therefore, if somewhat less valuable as a medical record, necessarily written in a manner more likely to interest an unlearned reader.

These letters, from a memorandum attached, appear to have been returned on the death of the professor, in 1819, to Dr. Hesselius. They are written, some in English, some in French, but the greater part in German. I am a faithful, though I am conscious, by no means a graceful translator, and although here and there I omit some passages, and shorten others, and disguise names, I have interpolated nothing.

CHAPTER I

Dr. Hesselius Relates How He Met
the Rev. Mr. Jennings

The Rev. Mr. Jennings is tall and thin. He is middle-aged, and dresses with a natty, old-fashioned, high-church precision. He is naturally a little stately, but not at all stiff. His features, without being handsome, are well formed, and their expression extremely kind, but also shy.

I met him one evening at Lady Mary Heyduke's. The modesty and benevolence of his countenance are extremely prepossessing.

We were but a small party, and he joined agreeably enough in the conversation, He seems to enjoy listening very much more than contributing to the talk; but what he says is always to the purpose and well said. He is a great favourite of Lady Mary's, who it seems, consults him upon many things, and thinks him the most happy and blessed person on earth. Little knows she about him.

The Rev. Mr. Jennings is a bachelor, and has, they say sixty thousand pounds in the funds. He is a charitable man. He is most anxious to be actively employed in his sacred profession, and yet though always tolerably well elsewhere, when he goes down to his vicarage in Warwickshire, to engage in the actual duties of his sacred calling, his health soon fails him, and in a very strange way. So says Lady Mary.

There is no doubt that Mr. Jennings' health does break down in, generally, a sudden and mysterious way, sometimes in the very act of officiating in his old and pretty church at Kenlis. It may be his heart, it may be his brain. But so it has happened three or four times, or oftener, that after proceeding a certain way in the service, he has on a sudden stopped short, and after a silence, apparently quite unable to resume, he has fallen into solitary, inaudible prayer, his hands and his eyes uplifted, and then pale as death, and in the agitation of a strange shame and horror, descended trembling, and got into the vestry-room, leaving his congregation, without explanation, to themselves. This occurred when his curate was absent. When he goes down to Kenlis now, he always takes care to provide a clergyman to share his duty, and to supply his place on the instant should he become thus suddenly incapacitated.

When Mr. Jennings breaks down quite, and beats a retreat from the vicarage, and returns to London, where, in a dark street off Piccadilly, he inhabits a very narrow house, Lady Mary says that he is always perfectly well. I have my own opinion about that. There are degrees of course. We shall see.

Mr. Jennings is a perfectly gentlemanlike man. People, however, remark something odd. There is an impression a little ambiguous. One thing which certainly contributes to it, people I think don't remember; or, perhaps, distinctly remark. But I did, almost immediately. Mr. Jennings has a way of looking sidelong upon the carpet, as if his eye followed the movements of something there. This, of course, is not always. It occurs now and then. But often enough to give a certain oddity, as I have said, to his manner, and in this glance travelling along the floor there is something both shy and anxious.

A medical philosopher, as you are good enough to call me, elaborating theories by the aid of cases sought out by himself, and by him watched and scrutinised with more time at command, and consequently infinitely more minuteness than the ordinary practitioner can afford, falls insensibly into habits of observation, which accompany him everywhere, and are exercised, as some people would say, impertinently, upon every subject that presents itself with the least likelihood of rewarding inquiry.

There was a promise of this kind in the slight, timid, kindly, but reserved gentleman, whom I met for the first time at this agreeable little evening gathering. I observed, of course, more than I here set down; but I reserve all that borders on the technical for a strictly scientific paper.

I may remark, that when I here speak of medical science, I do so, as I hope some day to see it more generally understood, in a much more comprehensive sense than its generally material treatment would warrant. I believe the entire natural world is but the ultimate expression of that spiritual world from which, and in which alone, it has its life. I believe that the essential man is a spirit, that the spirit is an organised substance, but as different in point of material from what we ordinarily understand by matter, as light or electricity is; that the material body is, in the most literal sense, a vesture, and death consequently no interruption of the living man's existence, but simply his extrication from the natural body —a process which commences at the moment of what we term death, and the completion of which, at furthest a few days later, is the resurrection "in power."

The person who weighs the consequences of these positions will probably see their practical bearing upon medical science. This is, however, by no means the proper place for displaying the proofs and discussing the consequences of this too generally unrecognized state of facts.

In pursuance of my habit, I was covertly observing Mr. Jennings, with all my caution—I think he perceived it—and I saw plainly that he was as cautiously observing me. Lady Mary happening to address me by my name, as Dr. Hesselius, I saw that he glanced at me more sharply, and then became thoughtful for a few minutes.

After this, as I conversed with a gentleman at the other end of the room, I saw him look at me more steadily, and with an interest which I thought I understood. I then saw him take an opportunity of chatting with Lady Mary, and was, as one always is, perfectly aware of being the subject of a distant inquiry and answer.

This tall clergyman approached me by-and-by; and in a little time we had got into conversation. When two people, who like reading, and know books and places, having travelled, wish to discourse, it is very strange if they can't find topics. It was not accident that brought him near me, and led him into conversation.

He knew German and had read my Essays on Metaphysical Medicine which suggest more than they actually say.

This courteous man, gentle, shy, plainly a man of thought and reading, who moving and talking among us, was not altogether of us, and whom I already suspected of leading a life whose transactions and alarms were carefully concealed, with an impenetrable reserve from, not only the world, but his best beloved friends—was cautiously weighing in his own mind the idea of taking a certain step with regard to me.

I penetrated his thoughts without his being aware of it, and was careful to say nothing which could betray to his sensitive vigilance my suspicions respecting his position, or my surmises about his plans respecting myself.

We chatted upon indifferent subjects for a time but at last he said:

"I was very much interested by some papers of yours, Dr. Hesselius, upon what you term Metaphysical Medicine—I read them in German, ten or twelve years ago—have they been translated?"

"No, I'm sure they have not—I should have heard. They would have asked my leave, I think."

"I asked the publishers here, a few months ago, to get the book for me in the original German; but they tell me it is out of print."

"So it is, and has been for some years; but it flatters me as an author to find that you have not forgotten my little book, although," I added, laughing, "ten or twelve years is a considerable time to have managed without it; but I suppose you have been turning the subject over again in your mind, or something has happened lately to revive your interest in it."

At this remark, accompanied by a glance of inquiry, a sudden embarrassment disturbed Mr. Jennings, analogous to that which makes a young lady blush and look foolish. He dropped his eyes, and folded his hands together uneasily, and looked oddly, and you would have said, guiltily, for a moment.

I helped him out of his awkwardness in the best way, by appearing not to observe it, and going straight on, I said: "Those revivals of interest in a subject happen to me often; one book suggests another, and often sends me back a wild-goose chase over an interval of twenty years. But if you still care to possess a copy, I shall be only too happy to provide you; I have still got two or three by me —and if you allow me to present one I shall be very much honoured."

"You are very good indeed," he said, quite at his ease again, in a moment: "I almost despaired—I don't know how to thank you."

"Pray don't say a word; the thing is really so little worth that I am only ashamed of having offered it, and if you thank me any more I shall throw it into the fire in a fit of modesty."

Mr. Jennings laughed. He inquired where I was staying in London, and after a little more conversation on a variety of subjects, he took his departure.

CHAPTER II

The Doctor Questions Lady Mary and She Answers

"I like your vicar so much, Lady Mary," said I, as soon as he was gone. "He has read, travelled, and thought, and having also suffered, he ought to be an accomplished companion."

"So he is, and, better still, he is a really good man," said she. "His advice is invaluable about my schools, and all my little undertakings at Dawlbridge, and he's so painstaking, he takes so much trouble—you have no idea—wherever he thinks he can be of use: he's so good-natured and so sensible."

"It is pleasant to hear so good an account of his neighbourly virtues. I can only testify to his being an agreeable and gentle companion, and in addition to what you have told me, I think I can tell you two or three things about him," said I.

"Really!"

"Yes, to begin with, he's unmarried."

"Yes, that's right—go on."

"He has been writing, that is he *was*, but for two or three years perhaps, he has not gone on with his work, and the book was upon some rather abstract subject—perhaps theology."

"Well, he was writing a book, as you say; I'm not quite sure what it was about, but only that it was nothing that I cared for; very likely you are right, and he certainly did stop—yes."

"And although he only drank a little coffee here to-night, he likes tea, at least, did like it extravagantly."

"Yes, that's *quite* true."

"He drank green tea, a good deal, didn't he?" I pursued.

"Well, that's very odd! Green tea was a subject on which we used almost to quarrel."

"But he has quite given that up," said I.

"So he has."

"And, now, one more fact. His mother or his father, did you know them?"

"Yes, both; his father is only ten years dead, and their place is near Dawlbridge. We knew them very well," she answered.

"Well, either his mother or his father—I should rather think his father, saw a ghost," said I.

"Well, you really are a conjurer, Dr. Hesselius."

"Conjurer or no, haven't I said right?" I answered merrily.

"You certainly have, and it *was* his father: he was a silent, whimsical man, and he used to bore my father about his dreams, and at last he told him a story about a ghost he had seen and talked with, and a very odd story it was. I remember it particularly, because I was so afraid of him. This story was long before he died—when I was quite a child—and his ways were so silent and moping, and he used to drop in sometimes, in the dusk, when I was alone in the drawing-room, and I used to fancy there were ghosts about him."

I smiled and nodded.

"And now, having established my character as a conjurer, I think I must say good-night," said I.

"But how *did* you find it out?"

"By the planets, of course, as the gipsies do," I answered, and so, gaily we said good-night.

Next morning I sent the little book he had been inquiring after, and a note to Mr. Jennings, and on returning late that evening, I found that he had called at my lodgings, and left his card. He asked whether I was at home, and asked at what hour he would be most likely to find me.

Does he intend opening his case, and consulting me "professionally," as they say? I hope so. I have already conceived a theory about him. It is supported by Lady Mary's answers to my parting questions. I should like much to ascertain from his own lips. But what can I do consistently with good breeding to invite a confession? Nothing. I rather think he meditates one. At all events, my dear Van L., I shan't make myself difficult of access; I mean to return his visit tomorrow. It will be only civil in return for his politeness, to ask to see him. Perhaps something may come of it. Whether much, little, or nothing, my dear Van L., you shall hear.

CHAPTER III

Dr. Hesselius Picks Up Something in Latin Books

Well, I have called at Blank Street.

On inquiring at the door, the servant told me that Mr. Jennings was engaged very particularly with a gentleman, a clergyman from Kenlis, his parish in the country. Intending to reserve my privilege, and to call again, I merely intimated that I should try another time, and had turned to go, when the servant begged my pardon, and asked me, looking at me a little more attentively than well-bred persons of his order usually do, whether I was Dr. Hesselius; and, on learning that I was, he said, "Perhaps then, sir, you would allow me to mention it to Mr. Jennings, for I am sure he wishes to see you."

The servant returned in a moment, with a message from Mr. Jennings, asking me to go into his study, which was in effect his back drawing-room, promising to be with me in a very few minutes.

This was really a study—almost a library. The room was lofty, with two tall slender windows, and rich dark curtains. It was much larger than I had expected, and stored with books on every side, from the floor to the ceiling. The upper carpet— for to my tread it felt that there were two or three—was a Turkey carpet. My steps fell noiselessly. The bookcases standing out, placed the windows, particularly narrow ones, in deep recesses. The effect of the room was, although extremely comfortable, and even luxurious, decidedly gloomy, and aided by the silence, almost oppressive. Perhaps, however, I ought to have allowed something for association. My mind had connected peculiar ideas with Mr. Jennings. I stepped into this perfectly silent room, of a very silent house, with a peculiar foreboding; and its darkness, and solemn clothing of books, for except where two narrow looking-glasses were set in the wall, they were everywhere, helped this somber feeling.

While awaiting Mr. Jennings' arrival, I amused myself by looking into some of the books with which his shelves were laden. Not among these, but immediately under them, with their backs upward, on the floor, I lighted upon a complete set of Swedenborg's "Arcana Cælestia," in the original Latin, a very fine folio set, bound in the natty livery which theology affects, pure vellum, namely, gold letters, and carmine edges. There were paper markers in several of these volumes, I raised and placed them, one after the other, upon the table, and opening where these papers were placed, I read in the solemn Latin phraseology, a series of sentences indicated by a pencilled line at the margin. Of these I copy here a few, translating them into English.

"When man's interior sight is opened, which is that of his spirit, then there appear the things of another life, which cannot possibly be made visible to the bodily sight." . . . .

"By the internal sight it has been granted me to see the things that are in the other life, more clearly than I see those that are in the world. From these considerations, it is evident that external vision exists from interior vision, and this from a vision still more interior, and so on." . . . .

"There are with every man at least two evil spirits." . . . .

"With wicked genii there is also a fluent speech, but harsh and grating. There is also among them a speech which is not fluent, wherein the dissent of the thoughts is perceived as something secretly creeping along within it."

"The evil spirits associated with man are, indeed from the hells, but when with man they are not then in hell, but are taken out thence. The place where they then are, is in the midst between heaven and hell, and is called the world of spirits—when the evil spirits who are with man, are in that world, they are not in any infernal torment, but in every thought and affection of man, and so, in all that the man himself enjoys. But when they are remitted into their hell, they return to their former state." . . . .

"If evil spirits could perceive that they were associated with man, and yet that they were spirits separate from him, and if they could flow in into the things of his body, they would attempt by a thousand means to destroy him; for they hate man with a deadly hatred." . . . .

"Knowing, therefore, that I was a man in the body, they were continually striving to destroy me, not as to the body only, but especially as to the soul; for to destroy any man or spirit is the very delight of the life of all who are in hell; but I have been continually protected by the Lord. Hence it appears how dangerous it is for man to be in a living consort with spirits, unless he be in the good of faith." . . . .

"Nothing is more carefully guarded from the knowledge of associate spirits than their being thus conjoint with a man, for if they knew it they would speak to him, with the intention to destroy him." . . . .

"The delight of hell is to do evil to man, and to hasten his eternal ruin."

A long note, written with a very sharp and fine pencil, in Mr. Jennings' neat hand, at the foot of the page, caught my eye. Expecting his criticism upon the text, I read a word or two, and stopped, for it was something quite different, and began with these words, *Deus misereatur mei*—"May God compassionate me." Thus warned of its private nature, I averted my eyes, and shut the book, replacing all the volumes as I had found them, except one which interested me, and in which, as men studious and solitary in their habits will do, I grew so absorbed as to take no cognisance of the outer world, nor to remember where I was.

I was reading some pages which refer to "representatives" and "correspondents," in the technical language of Swedenborg, and had arrived at a passage, the substance of which is, that evil spirits, when seen by other eyes than those of their infernal associates, present themselves, by "correspondence," in the shape of the beast (*fera*) which represents their particular lust and life, in aspect direful and atrocious. This is a long passage, and particularises a number of those bestial forms.

CHAPTER IV

Four Eyes Were Reading the Passage

I was running the head of my pencil-case along the line as I read it, and something caused me to raise my eyes.

Directly before me was one of the mirrors I have mentioned, in which I saw reflected the tall shape of my friend, Mr. Jennings, leaning over my shoulder, and reading the page at which I was busy, and with a face so dark and wild that I should hardly have known him.

I turned and rose. He stood erect also, and with an effort laughed a little, saying:

"I came in and asked you how you did, but without succeeding in awaking you from your book; so I could not restrain my curiosity, and very impertinently, I'm afraid, peeped over your shoulder. This is not your first time of looking into those pages. You have looked into Swedenborg, no doubt, long ago?"

"Oh dear, yes! I owe Swedenborg a great deal; you will discover traces of him in the little book on Metaphysical Medicine, which you were so good as to remember."

Although my friend affected a gaiety of manner, there was a slight flush in his face, and I could perceive that he was inwardly much perturbed.

"I'm scarcely yet qualified, I know so little of Swedenborg. I've only had them a fortnight," he answered, "and I think they are rather likely to make a solitary man nervous—that is, judging from the very little I have read—I don't say that they have made me so," he laughed; "and I'm so very much obliged for the book. I hope you got my note?"

I made all proper acknowledgments and modest disclaimers.

"I never read a book that I go with, so entirely, as that of yours," he continued. "I saw at once there is more in it than is quite unfolded. Do you know Dr. Harley?" he asked, rather abruptly.

In passing, the editor remarks that the physician here named was one of the most eminent who had ever practised in England.

I did, having had letters to him, and had experienced from him great courtesy and considerable assistance during my visit to England.

"I think that man one of the very greatest fools I ever met in my life," said Mr. Jennings.

This was the first time I had ever heard him say a sharp thing of anybody, and such a term applied to so high a name a little startled me.

"Really! and in what way?" I asked.

"In his profession," he answered.

I smiled.

"I mean this," he said: "he seems to me, one half, blind—I mean one half of all he looks at is dark—preternaturally bright and vivid all the rest; and the worst of it is, it seems *wilful*. I can't get him—I mean he won't—I've had some experience of him as a physician, but I look on him as, in that sense, no better than a paralytic mind, an intellect half dead. I'll tell you—I know I shall some time—all about it," he said, with a little agitation. "You stay some months longer in England. If I should be out of town during your stay for a little time, would you allow me to trouble you with a letter?"

"I should be only too happy," I assured him.

"Very good of you. I am so utterly dissatisfied with Harley."

"A little leaning to the materialistic school," I said.

"A *mere* materialist," he corrected me; "you can't think how that sort of thing worries one who knows better. You won't tell any one—any of my friends you know—that I am hippish; now, for instance, no one knows—not even Lady Mary—that I have seen Dr. Harley, or any other doctor. So pray don't mention it; and, if I should have any threatening of an attack, you'll kindly let me write, or, should I be in town, have a little talk with you."

I was full of conjecture, and unconsciously I found I had fixed my eyes gravely on him, for he lowered his for a moment, and he said:

"I see you think I might as well tell you now, or else you are forming a conjecture; but you may as well give it up. If you were guessing all the rest of your life, you will never hit on it."

He shook his head smiling, and over that wintry sunshine a black cloud suddenly came down, and he drew his breath in, through his teeth as men do in pain.

"Sorry, of course, to learn that you apprehend occasion to consult any of us; but, command me when and how you like, and I need not assure you that your confidence is sacred."

He then talked of quite other things, and in a comparatively cheerful way and after a little time, I took my leave.

CHAPTER V

Dr. Hesselius is Summoned to Richmond

We parted cheerfully, but he was not cheerful, nor was I. There are certain expressions of that powerful organ of spirit—the human face—which, although I have seen them often, and possess a doctor's nerve, yet disturb me profoundly. One look of Mr. Jennings haunted me. It had seized my imagination with so dismal a power that I changed my plans for the evening, and went to the opera, feeling that I wanted a change of ideas.

I heard nothing of or from him for two or three days, when a note in his hand reached me. It was cheerful, and full of hope. He said that he had been for some little time so much better—quite well, in fact—that he was going to make a little experiment, and run down for a month or so to his parish, to try whether a little work might not quite set him up. There was in it a fervent religious expression of gratitude for his restoration, as he now almost hoped he might call it.

A day or two later I saw Lady Mary, who repeated what his note had announced, and told me that he was actually in Warwickshire, having resumed his clerical duties at Kenlis; and she added, "I begin to think that he is really perfectly well, and that there never was anything the matter, more than nerves and fancy; we are all nervous, but I fancy there is nothing like a little hard work for that kind of weakness, and he has made up his mind to try it. I should not be surprised if he did not come back for a year."

Notwithstanding all this confidence, only two days later I had this note, dated from his house off Piccadilly:

DEAR SIR,—I have returned disappointed. If I should feel at all able to see you, I shall write to ask you kindly to call. At present, I am too low, and, in fact, simply unable to say all I wish to say. Pray don't mention my name to my friends. I can see no one. By-and-by, please God, you shall hear from me. I mean to take a run into Shropshire, where some of my people are. God bless you! May we, on my return, meet more happily than I can now write.

About a week after this I saw Lady Mary at her own house, the last person, she said, left in town, and just on the wing for Brighton, for the London season was quite over. She told me that she had heard from Mr. Jenning's niece, Martha, in Shropshire. There was nothing to be gathered from her letter, more than that he was low and nervous. In those words, of which healthy people think so lightly, what a world of suffering is sometimes hidden!

Nearly five weeks had passed without any further news of Mr. Jennings. At the end of that time I received a note from him. He wrote:

"I have been in the country, and have had change of air, change of scene, change of faces, change of everything—and in everything —but *myself*. I have made up my mind, so far as the most irresolute creature on earth can do it, to tell my case fully to you. If your engagements will permit, pray come to me to-day, to-morrow, or the next day; but, pray defer as little as possible. You know not how much I need help. I have a quiet house at Richmond, where I now am. Perhaps you can manage to come to dinner, or to luncheon, or even to tea. You shall have no trouble in finding me out. The servant at Blank Street, who takes this note, will have a carriage at your door at any hour you please; and I am always to be found. You will say that I ought not to be alone. I have tried everything. Come and see."

I called up the servant, and decided on going out the same evening, which accordingly I did.

He would have been much better in a lodging-house, or hotel, I thought, as I drove up through a short double row of sombre elms to a very old-fashioned brick house, darkened by the foliage of these trees, which overtopped, and nearly surrounded it. It was a perverse choice, for nothing could be imagined more triste and silent. The house, I found, belonged to him. He had stayed for a day or two in town, and, finding it for some cause insupportable, had come out here, probably because being furnished and his own, he was relieved of the thought and delay of selection, by coming here.

The sun had already set, and the red reflected light of the western sky illuminated the scene with the peculiar effect with which we are all familiar. The hall seemed very dark, but, getting to the back drawing-room, whose windows command the west, I was again in the same dusky light.

I sat down, looking out upon the richly-wooded landscape that glowed in the grand and melancholy light which was every moment fading. The corners of the room were already dark; all was growing dim, and the gloom was insensibly toning my mind, already prepared for what was sinister. I was waiting alone for his arrival, which soon took place. The door communicating with the front room opened, and the tall figure of Mr. Jennings, faintly seen in the ruddy twilight, came, with quiet stealthy steps, into the room.

We shook hands, and, taking a chair to the window, where there was still light enough to enable us to see each other's faces, he sat down beside me, and, placing his hand upon my arm, with scarcely a word of preface began his narrative.

CHAPTER VI

How Mr. Jennings Met His Companion

The faint glow of the west, the pomp of the then lonely woods of Richmond, were before us, behind and about us the darkening room, and on the stony face of the sufferer—for the character of his face, though still gentle and sweet, was changed—rested that dim, odd glow which seems to descend and produce, where it touches, lights, sudden though faint, which are lost, almost without gradation, in darkness. The silence, too, was utter: not a distant wheel, or bark, or whistle from without; and within the depressing stillness of an invalid bachelor's house.

I guessed well the nature, though not even vaguely the particulars of the revelations I was about to receive, from that fixed face of suffering that so oddly flushed stood out, like a portrait of Schalken's, before its background of darkness.

"It began," he said, "on the 15th of October, three years and eleven weeks ago, and two days—I keep very accurate count, for every day is torment. If I leave anywhere a chasm in my narrative tell me.

"About four years ago I began a work, which had cost me very much thought and reading. It was upon the religious metaphysics of the ancients."

"I know," said I, "the actual religion of educated and thinking paganism, quite apart from symbolic worship? A wide and very interesting field."

"Yes, but not good for the mind—the Christian mind, I mean. Paganism is all bound together in essential unity, and, with evil sympathy, their religion involves their art, and both their manners, and the subject is a degrading fascination and the Nemesis sure. God forgive me!

"I wrote a great deal; I wrote late at night. I was always thinking on the subject, walking about, wherever I was, everywhere. It thoroughly infected me. You are to remember that all the material ideas connected with it were more or less of the beautiful, the subject itself delightfully interesting, and I, then, without a care."

He sighed heavily.

"I believe, that every one who sets about writing in earnest does his work, as a friend of mine phrased it, *on* something—tea, or coffee, or tobacco. I suppose there is a material waste that must be hourly supplied in such occupations, or that we should grow too abstracted, and the mind, as it were, pass out of the body, unless it were reminded often enough of the connection by actual sensation. At all events, I felt the want, and I supplied it. Tea was my companion—at first the ordinary black tea, made in the usual way, not too strong: but I drank a good deal, and increased its strength as I went on. I never experienced an uncomfortable symptom from it. I began to take a little green tea. I found the effect pleasanter, it cleared and intensified the power of thought so, I had come to take it frequently, but not stronger than one might take it for pleasure. I wrote a great deal out here, it was so quiet, and in this room. I used to sit up very late, and it became a habit with me to sip my tea—green tea—every now and then as my work proceeded. I had a little kettle on my table, that swung over a lamp, and made tea two or three times between eleven o'clock and two or three in the morning, my hours of going to bed. I used to go into town every day. I was not a monk, and, although I spent an hour or two in a library, hunting up authorities and looking out lights upon my theme, I was in no morbid state as far as I can judge. I met my friends pretty much as usual and enjoyed their society, and, on the whole, existence had never been, I think, so pleasant before.

"I had met with a man who had some odd old books, German editions in mediæval Latin, and I was only too happy to be permitted access to them. This obliging person's books were in the City, a very out-of-the-way part of it. I had rather out-stayed my intended hour, and, on coming out, seeing no cab near, I was tempted to get into the omnibus which used to drive past this house. It was darker than this by the time the 'bus had reached an old house, you may have remarked, with four poplars at each side of the door, and there the last passenger but myself got out. We drove along rather faster. It was twilight now. I leaned back in my corner next the door ruminating pleasantly.

"The interior of the omnibus was nearly dark. I had observed in the corner opposite to me at the other side, and at the end next the horses, two small circular reflections, as it seemed to me of a reddish light. They were about two inches apart, and about the size of those small brass buttons that yachting men used to put upon their jackets. I began to speculate, as listless men will, upon this trifle, as it seemed. From what centre did that faint but deep red light come, and from what—glass beads, buttons, toy decorations—was it reflected? We were lumbering along gently, having nearly a mile still to go. I had not solved the puzzle, and it became in another minute more odd, for these two luminous points, with a sudden jerk, descended nearer and nearer the floor, keeping still their relative distance and horizontal position, and then, as suddenly, they rose to the level of the seat on which I was sitting and I saw them no more.

"My curiosity was now really excited, and, before I had time to think, I saw again these two dull lamps, again together near the floor; again they disappeared, and again in their old corner I saw them.

"So, keeping my eyes upon them, I edged quietly up my own side, towards the end at which I still saw these tiny discs of red.

"There was very little light in the 'bus. It was nearly dark. I leaned forward to aid my endeavour to discover what these little circles really were. They shifted position a little as I did so. I began now to perceive an outline of something black, and I soon saw, with tolerable distinctness, the outline of a small black monkey, pushing its face forward in mimicry to meet mine; those were its eyes, and I now dimly saw its teeth grinning at me.

"I drew back, not knowing whether it might not meditate a spring. I fancied that one of the passengers had forgot this ugly pet, and wishing to ascertain something of its temper, though not caring to trust my fingers to it, I poked my umbrella softly towards it. It remained immovable—up to it—*through* it. For through it, and back and forward it passed, without the slightest resistance.

"I can't, in the least, convey to you the kind of horror that I felt. When I had ascertained that the thing was an illusion, as I then supposed, there came a misgiving about myself and a terror that fascinated me in impotence to remove my gaze from the eyes of the brute for some moments. As I looked, it made a little skip back, quite into the corner, and I, in a panic, found myself at the door, having put my head out, drawing deep breaths of the outer air, and staring at the lights and tress we were passing, too glad to reassure myself of reality.

"I stopped the 'bus and got out. I perceived the man look oddly at me as I paid him. I dare say there was something unusual in my looks and manner, for I had never felt so strangely before."

CHAPTER VII

The Journey: First Stage

"When the omnibus drove on, and I was alone upon the road, I looked carefully round to ascertain whether the monkey had followed me. To my indescribable relief I saw it nowhere. I can't describe easily what a shock I had received, and my sense of genuine gratitude on finding myself, as I supposed, quite rid of it.

"I had got out a little before we reached this house, two or three hundred steps. A brick wall runs along the footpath, and inside the wall is a hedge of yew, or some dark evergreen of that kind, and within that again the row of fine trees which you may have remarked as you came.

"This brick wall is about as high as my shoulder, and happening to raise my eyes I saw the monkey, with that stooping gait, on all fours, walking or creeping, close beside me, on top of the wall. I stopped, looking at it with a feeling of loathing and horror. As I stopped so did it. It sat up on the wall with its long hands on its knees looking at me. There was not light enough to see it much more than in outline, nor was it dark enough to bring the peculiar light of its eyes into strong relief. I still saw, however, that red foggy light plainly enough. It did not show its teeth, nor exhibit any sign of irritation, but seemed jaded and sulky, and was observing me steadily.

"I drew back into the middle of the road. It was an unconscious recoil, and there I stood, still looking at it. It did not move.

"With an instinctive determination to try something—anything, I turned about and walked briskly towards town with askance look, all the time, watching the movements of the beast. It crept swiftly along the wall, at exactly my pace.

"Where the wall ends, near the turn of the road, it came down, and with a wiry spring or two brought itself close to my feet, and continued to keep up with me, as I quickened my pace. It was at my left side, so close to my leg that I felt every moment as if I should tread upon it.

"The road was quite deserted and silent, and it was darker every moment. I stopped dismayed and bewildered, turning as I did so, the other way—I mean, towards this house, away from which I had been walking. When I stood still, the monkey drew back to a distance of, I suppose, about five or six yards, and remained stationary, watching me.

"I had been more agitated than I have said. I had read, of course, as everyone has, something about 'spectral illusions,' as you physicians term the phenomena of such cases. I considered my situation, and looked my misfortune in the face.

"These affections, I had read, are sometimes transitory and sometimes obstinate. I had read of cases in which the appearance, at first harmless, had, step by step, degenerated into something direful and insupportable, and ended by wearing its victim out. Still as I stood there, but for my bestial companion, quite alone, I tried to comfort myself by repeating again and again the assurance, 'the thing is purely disease, a well-known physical affection, as distinctly as small-pox or neuralgia. Doctors are all agreed on that, philosophy demonstrates it. I must not be a fool. I've been sitting up too late, and I daresay my digestion is quite wrong, and, with God's help, I shall be all right, and this is but a symptom of nervous dyspepsia.' Did I believe all this? Not one word of it, no more than any other miserable being ever did who is once seized and riveted in this satanic captivity. Against my convictions, I might say my knowledge, I was simply bullying myself into a false courage.

"I now walked homeward. I had only a few hundred yards to go. I had forced myself into a sort of resignation, but I had not got over the sickening shock and the flurry of the first certainty of my misfortune.

"I made up my mind to pass the night at home. The brute moved close beside me, and I fancied there was the sort of anxious drawing toward the house, which one sees in tired horses or dogs, sometimes as they come toward home.

"I was afraid to go into town, I was afraid of any one's seeing and recognizing me. I was conscious of an irrepressible agitation in my manner. Also, I was afraid of any violent change in my habits, such as going to a place of amusement, or walking from home in order to fatigue myself. At the hall door it waited till I mounted the steps, and when the door was opened entered with me.

"I drank no tea that night. I got cigars and some brandy and water. My idea was that I should act upon my material system, and by living for a while in sensation apart from thought, send myself forcibly, as it were, into a new groove. I came up here to this drawing-room. I sat just here. The monkey then got upon a small table that then stood *there*. It looked dazed and languid. An irrepressible uneasiness as to its movements kept my eyes always upon it. Its eyes were half closed, but I could see them glow. It was looking steadily at me. In all situations, at all hours, it is awake and looking at me. That never changes.

"I shall not continue in detail my narrative of this particular night. I shall describe, rather, the phenomena of the first year, which never varied, essentially. I shall describe the monkey as it appeared in daylight. In the dark, as you shall presently hear, there are peculiarities. It is a small monkey, perfectly black. It had only one peculiarity—a character of malignity—unfathomable malignity. During the first year it looked sullen and sick. But this character of intense malice and vigilance was always underlying that surly languor. During all that time it acted as if on a plan of giving me as little trouble as was consistent with watching me. Its eyes were never off me. I have never lost sight of it, except in my sleep, light or dark, day or night, since it came here, excepting when it withdraws for some weeks at a time, unaccountably.

"In total dark it is visible as in daylight. I do not mean merely its eyes. It is *all* visible distinctly in a halo that resembles a glow of red embers, and which accompanies it in all its movements.

"When it leaves me for a time, it is always at night, in the dark, and in the same way. It grows at first uneasy, and then furious, and then advances towards me, grinning and shaking, its paws clenched, and, at the same time, there comes the appearance of fire in the grate. I never have any fire. I can't sleep in the room where there is any, and it draws nearer and nearer to the chimney, quivering, it seems, with rage, and when its fury rises to the highest pitch, it springs into the grate, and up the chimney, and I see it no more.

"When first this happened, I thought I was released. I was now a new man. A day passed—a night—and no return, and a blessed week—a week—another week. I was always on my knees, Dr. Hesselius, always, thanking God and praying. A whole month passed of liberty, but on a sudden, it was with me again."

CHAPTER VIII

The Second Stage

"It was with me, and the malice which before was torpid under a sullen exterior, was now active. It was perfectly unchanged in every other respect. This new energy was apparent in its activity and its looks, and soon in other ways.

"For a time, you will understand, the change was shown only in an increased vivacity, and an air of menace, as if it were always brooding over some atrocious plan. Its eyes, as before, were never off me."

"Is it here now?" I asked.

"No," he replied, "it has been absent exactly a fortnight and a day—fifteen days. It has sometimes been away so long as nearly two months, once for three. Its absence always exceeds a fortnight, although it may be but by a single day. Fifteen days having past since I saw it last, it may return now at any moment."

"Is its return," I asked, "accompanied by any peculiar manifestation?"

"Nothing—no," he said. "It is simply with me again. On lifting my eyes from a book, or turning my head, I see it, as usual, looking at me, and then it remains, as before, for its appointed time. I have never told so much and so minutely before to any one."

I perceived that he was agitated, and looking like death, and he repeatedly applied his handkerchief to his forehead; I suggested that he might be tired, and told him that I would call, with pleasure, in the morning, but he said:

"No, if you don't mind hearing it all now. I have got so far, and I should prefer making one effort of it. When I spoke to Dr. Harley, I had nothing like so much to tell. You are a philosophic physician. You give spirit its proper rank. If this thing is real——"

He paused looking at me with agitated inquiry.

"We can discuss it by-and-by, and very fully. I will give you all I think," I answered, after an interval.

"Well—very well. If it is anything real, I say, it is prevailing, little by little, and drawing me more interiorly into hell. Optic nerves, he talked of. Ah! well—there are other nerves of communication. May God Almighty help me! You shall hear.

"Its power of action, I tell you, had increased. Its malice became, in a way, aggressive. About two years ago, some questions that were pending between me and the bishop having been settled, I went down to my parish in Warwickshire, anxious to find occupation in my profession. I was not prepared for what happened, although I have since thought I might have apprehended something like it. The reason of my saying so is this——"

He was beginning to speak with a great deal more effort and reluctance, and sighed often, and seemed at times nearly overcome. But at this time his manner was not agitated. It was more like that of a sinking patient, who has given himself up.

"Yes, but I will first tell you about Kenlis, my parish.

"It was with me when I left this place for Dawlbridge. It was my silent travelling companion, and it remained with me at the vicarage. When I entered on the discharge of my duties, another change took place. The thing exhibited an atrocious determination to thwart me. It was with me in the church—in the reading-desk—in the pulpit—within the communion rails. At last, it reached this extremity, that while I was reading to the congregation, it would spring upon the book and squat there, so that I was unable to see the page. This happened more than once.

"I left Dawlbridge for a time. I placed myself in Dr. Harley's hands. I did everything he told me. He gave my case a great deal of thought. It interested him, I think. He seemed successful. For nearly three months I was perfectly free from a return. I began to think I was safe. With his full assent I returned to Dawlbridge.

"I travelled in a chaise. I was in good spirits. I was more—I was happy and grateful. I was returning, as I thought, delivered from a dreadful hallucination, to the scene of duties which I longed to enter upon. It was a beautiful sunny evening, everything looked serene and cheerful, and I was delighted. I remember looking out of the window to see the spire of my church at Kenlis among the trees, at the point where one has the earliest view of it. It is exactly where the little stream that bounds the parish passes under the road by a culvert, and where it emerges at the road-side, a stone with an old inscription is placed. As we passed this point, I drew my head in and sat down, and in the corner of the chaise was the monkey.

"For a moment I felt faint, and then quite wild with despair and horror. I called to the driver, and got out, and sat down at the road-side, and prayed to God silently for mercy. A despairing resignation supervened. My companion was with me as I re-entered the vicarage. The same persecution followed. After a short struggle I submitted, and soon I left the place.

"I told you," he said," that the beast has before this become in certain ways aggressive. I will explain a little. It seemed to be ac-tuated by intense and increasing fury, whenever I said my prayers, or even meditated prayer. It amounted at last to a dreadful inter-ruption. You will ask, how could a silent immaterial phantom effect that? It was thus, whenever I meditated praying; It was al-ways before me, and nearer and nearer.

"It used to spring on a table, on the back of a chair, on the chimney-piece, and slowly to swing itself from side to side, looking at me all the time. There is in its motion an indefinable power to dissipate thought, and to contract one's attention to that monot-ony, till the ideas shrink, as it were, to a point, and at last to noth-ing—and unless I had started up, and shook off the catalepsy I have felt as if my mind were on the point of losing itself. There are other ways," he sighed heavily; "thus, for instance, while I pray with my eyes closed, it comes closer and closer, and I see it. I know it is not to be accounted for physically, but I do actually see it, though my lids are closed, and so it rocks my mind, as it were, and overpowers me, and I am obliged to rise from my knees. If you had ever yourself known this, you would be acquainted with desperation."

CHAPTER IX

The Third Stage

"I see, Dr. Hesselius, that you don't lose one word of my statement.

I need not ask you to listen specially to what I am now going to tell you. They talk of the optic nerves, and of spectral illusions, as if the organ of sight was the only point assailable by the influences that have fastened upon me—I know better. For two years in my direful case that limitation prevailed. But as food is taken in softly at the lips, and then brought under the teeth, as the tip of the little finger caught in a mill crank will draw in the hand, and the arm, and the whole body, so the miserable mortal who has been once caught firmly by the end of the finest fibre of his nerve, is drawn in and in, by the enormous machinery of hell, until he is as I am. Yes, Doctor, as *I* am, for a while I talk to you, and implore relief, I feel that my prayer is for the impossible, and my pleading with the inexorable."

I endeavoured to calm his visibly increasing agitation, and told him that he must not despair.

While we talked the night had overtaken us. The filmy moonlight was wide over the scene which the window commanded, and I said:

"Perhaps you would prefer having candles. This light, you know, is odd. I should wish you, as much as possible, under your usual conditions while I make my diagnosis, shall I call it—otherwise I don't care."

"All lights are the same to me," he said; "except when I read or write, I care not if night were perpetual. I am going to tell you what happened about a year ago. The thing began to speak to me."

"Speak! How do you mean—speak as a man does, do you mean?"

"Yes; speak in words and consecutive sentences, with perfect coherence and articulation; but there is a peculiarity. It is not like the tone of a human voice. It is not by my ears it reaches me—it comes like a singing through my head.

"This faculty, the power of speaking to me, will be my undoing. It won't let me pray, it interrupts me with dreadful blasphemies. I dare not go on, I could not. Oh! Doctor, can the skill, and thought, and prayers of man avail me nothing!"

"You must promise me, my dear sir, not to trouble yourself with unnecessarily exciting thoughts; confine yourself strictly to the narrative of *facts;* and recollect, above all, that even if the thing that infests you be, you seem to suppose a reality with an actual independent life and will, yet it can have no power to hurt you, unless it be given from above: its access to your senses depends mainly upon your physical condition—this is, under God, your comfort and reliance: we are all alike environed. It is only that in your case, the *'paries,'* the veil of the flesh, the screen, is a little out of repair, and sights and sounds are transmitted. We must enter on a new course, sir,—be encouraged. I'll give to-night to the careful consideration of the whole case."

"You are very good, sir; you think it worth trying, you don't give me quite up; but, sir, you don't know, it is gaining such an influence over me: it orders me about, it is such a tyrant, and I'm growing so helpless. May God deliver me!"

"It orders you about—of course you mean by speech?"

"Yes, yes; it is always urging me to crimes, to injure others, or myself. You see, Doctor, the situation is urgent, it is indeed. When I was in Shropshire, a few weeks ago" (Mr. Jennings was speaking rapidly and trembling now, holding my arm with one hand, and looking in my face), "I went out one day with a party of friends for a walk: my persecutor, I tell you, was with me at the time. I lagged behind the rest: the country near the Dee, you know, is beautiful. Our path happened to lie near a coal mine, and at the verge of the wood is a perpendicular shaft, they say, a hundred and fifty feet deep. My niece had remained behind with me—she knows, of course nothing of the nature of my sufferings. She knew, however, that I had been ill, and was low, and she remained to prevent my being quite alone. As we loitered slowly on together, the brute that accompanied me was urging me to throw myself down the shaft. I tell you now—oh, sir, think of it!—the one consideration that saved me from that hideous death was the fear lest the shock of witnessing the occurrence should be too much for the poor girl. I asked her to go on and walk with her friends, saying that I could go no further. She made excuses, and the more I urged her the firmer she became. She looked doubtful and frightened. I suppose there was something in my looks or manner that alarmed her; but she would not go, and that literally saved me. You had no idea, sir, that a living man could be made so abject a slave of Satan," he said, with a ghastly groan and a shudder.

There was a pause here, and I said, "You *were* preserved nevertheless. It was the act of God. You are in His hands and in the power of no other being: be therefore confident for the future."

CHAPTER X

Home

I made him have candles lighted, and saw the room looking

cheery and inhabited before I left him. I told him that he must regard his illness strictly as one dependent on physical, though *subtle* physical causes. I told him that he had evidence of God's care and love in the deliverance which he had just described, and that I had perceived with pain that he seemed to regard its peculiar features as indicating that he had been delivered over to spiritual reprobation. Than such a conclusion nothing could be, I insisted, less warranted; and not only so, but more contrary to facts, as disclosed in his mysterious deliverance from that murderous influence during his Shropshire excursion. First, his niece had been retained by his side without his intending to keep her near him; and, secondly, there had been infused into his mind an irresistible repugnance to execute the dreadful suggestion in her presence.

As I reasoned this point with him, Mr. Jennings wept. He seemed comforted. One promise I exacted, which was that should the monkey at any time return, I should be sent for immediately; and, repeating my assurance that I would give neither time nor thought to any other subject until I had thoroughly investigated his case, and that to-morrow he should hear the result, I took my leave.

Before getting into the carriage I told the servant that his master was far from well, and that he should make a point of frequently looking into his room.

My own arrangements I made with a view to being quite secure from interruption.

I merely called at my lodgings, and with a travelling-desk and carpet-bag, set off in a hackney carriage for an inn about two miles out of town, called "The Horns," a very quiet and comfortable house, with good thick walls. And there I resolved, without the possibility of intrusion or distraction, to devote some hours of the the night, in my comfortable sitting-room, to Mr. Jennings' case, and so much of the morning as it might require.

(There occurs here a careful note of Dr. Hesselius' opinion upon the case, and of the habits, dietary, and medicines which he prescribed. It is curious—some persons would say mystical. But, on the whole, I doubt whether it would sufficiently interest a reader of the kind I am likely to meet with, to warrant its being here reprinted. The whole letter was plainly written at the inn where he had hid himself for the occasion. The next letter is dated from his town lodgings.)

I left town for the inn where I slept last night at half-past nine, and did not arrive at my room in town until one o'clock this afternoon. I found a letter in Mr. Jennings' hand upon my table. It had not come by post, and, on inquiry, I learned that Mr. Jennings' servant had brought it, and on learning that I was not to return until to-day, and that no one could tell him my address, he seemed very uncomfortable, and said his orders from his master were that that he was not to return without an answer.

I opened the letter and read:

DEAR DR. HESSELIUS.—It is here. You had not been an hour gone when it returned. It is speaking. It knows all that has happened. It knows everything—it knows you, and is frantic and atrocious. It reviles. I send you this. It knows every word I have written—I write. This I promised, and I therefore write, but I fear very confused, very incoherently. I am so interrupted, disturbed.

Ever yours, sincerely yours,
ROBERT LYNDER JENNINGS.

"When did this come?" I asked.

"About eleven last night: the man was here again, and has been here three times to-day. The last time is about an hour since."

Thus answered, and with the notes I had made upon his case in my pocket, I was in a few minutes driving towards Richmond, to see Mr. Jennings.

I by no means, as you perceive, despaired of Mr. Jennings' case. He had himself remembered and applied, though quite in a mistaken way, the principle which I lay down in my Metaphysical Medicine, and which governs all such cases. I was about to apply it in earnest. I was profoundly interested, and very anxious to see and examine him while the "enemy" was actually present.

I drove up to the sombre house, and ran up the steps, and knocked. The door, in a little time, was opened by a tall woman in black silk. She looked ill, and as if she had been crying. She curtseyed, and heard my question, but she did not answer. She turned her face away, extending her hand towards two men who were coming down-stairs; and thus having, as it were, tacitly made me over to them, she passed through a side-door hastily and shut it.

The man who was nearest the hall, I at once accosted, but being now close to him, I was shocked to see that both his hands were covered with blood.

I drew back a little, and the man, passing downstairs, merely said in a low tone, "Here's the servant, sir."

The servant had stopped on the stairs, confounded and dumb at seeing me. He was rubbing his hands in a handkerchief, and it was steeped in blood.

"Jones, what is it? what has happened?" I asked, while a sickening suspicion overpowered me.

The man asked me to come up to the lobby. I was beside him in a moment, and, frowning and pallid, with contracted eyes, he told me the horror which I already half guessed.

His master had made away with himself.

I went upstairs with him to the room—what I saw there I won't tell you. He had cut his throat with his razor. It was a frightful gash. The two men had laid him on the bed, and composed his limbs. It had happened, as the immense pool of blood on the floor declared, at some distance between the bed and the window. There was carpet round his bed, and a carpet under his dressing-table, but none on the rest of the floor, for the man said he did not like a carpet on his bedroom. In this sombre and now terrible room, one of the great elms that darkened the house was slowly moving the shadow of one of its great boughs upon this dreadful floor.

I beckoned to the servant, and we went downstairs together. I turned off the hall into an old-fashioned panelled room, and there standing, I heard all the servant had to tell. It was not a great deal.

"I concluded, sir, from your words, and looks, sir, as you left last night, that you thought my master was seriously ill. I thought it might be that you were afraid of a fit, or something. So I attended very close to your directions. He sat up late, till past three o'clock. He was not writing or reading. He was talking a great deal to himself, but that was nothing unusual. At about that hour I assisted him to undress, and left him in his slippers and dressing-gown. I went back softly in about half-an-hour. He was in his bed, quite undressed, and a pair of candles lighted on the table beside his bed. He was leaning on his elbow, and looking out at the other side of the bed when I came in. I asked him if he wanted anything, and he said No.

"I don't know whether it was what you said to me, sir, or something a little unusual about him, but I was uneasy, uncommon uneasy about him last night.

"In another half hour, or it might be a little more, I went up again. I did not hear him talking as before. I opened the door a little. The candles were both out, which was not usual. I had a bedroom candle, and I let the light in, a little bit, looking softly round. I saw him sitting in that chair beside the dressing-table with his clothes on again. He turned round and looked at me. I thought it strange he should get up and dress, and put out the candles to sit in the dark, that way. But I only asked him again if I could do anything for him. He said, No, rather sharp, I thought. I asked him if I might light the candles, and he said, 'Do as you like, Jones.' So I lighted them, and I lingered about the room, and he said, 'Tell me truth, Jones; why did you come again—you did not hear anyone cursing?' 'No, sir,' I said, wondering what he could mean.

" 'No,' said he, after me, 'of course, no;' and I said to him, 'Wouldn't it be well, sir, you went to bed? It's just five o'clock;' and he said nothing, but, 'Very likely; good-night, Jones.' So I went, sir, but in less than an hour I came again. The door was fast, and he heard me, and called as I thought from the bed to know what I wanted, and he desired me not to disturb him again. I lay down and slept for a little. It must have been between six and seven when I went up again. The door was still fast, and he made no answer, so I did not like to disturb him, and thinking he was asleep, I left him till nine. It was his custom to ring when he wished me to come, and I had no particular hour for calling him. I tapped very gently, and getting no answer, I stayed away a good while, supposing he was getting some rest then. It was not till eleven o'clock I grew really uncomfortable about him—for at the latest he was never, that I could remember, later than half-past ten. I got no answer. I knocked and called, and still no answer. So not being able to force the door, I called Thomas from the stables, and together we forced it, and found him in the shocking way you saw."

Jones had no more to tell. Poor Mr. Jennings was very gentle, and very kind. All his people were fond of him. I could see that the servant was very much moved.

So, dejected and agitated, I passed from that terrible house, and its dark canopy of elms, and I hope I shall never see it more. While I write to you I feel like a man who has but half waked from a frightful and monotonous dream. My memory rejects the picture with incredulity and horror. Yet I know it is true. It is the story of the process of a poison, a poison which excites the reciprocal action of spirit and nerve, and paralyses the tissue that separates those cognate functions of the senses, the external and the interior. Thus we find strange bed-fellows, and the mortal and immortal prematurely make acquaintance.

CONCLUSION

A Word for Those Who Suffer

My dear Van L—, you have suffered from an affection similar to that which I have just described. You twice complained of a return of it.

Who, under God, cured you? Your humble servant, Martin Hesselius. Let me rather adopt the more emphasised piety of a certain good old French surgeon of three hundred years ago: "I treated, and God cured you."

Come, my friend, you are not to be hippish. Let me tell you a fact.

I have met with, and treated, as my book shows, fifty-seven cases of this kind of vision, which I term indifferently "sublimated," "precocious," and "interior."

There is another class of affections which are truly termed—though commonly confounded with those which I describe—spectral illusions. These latter I look upon as being no less simply curable than a cold in the head or a trifling dyspepsia.

It is those which rank in the first category that test our promptitude of thought. Fifty-seven such cases have I encounteed, neither more nor less. And in how many of these have I failed? In no one single instance.

There is no one affliction of mortality more easily and certainly reducible, with a little patience, and a rational confidence in the physician. With these simple conditions, I look upon the cure as absolutely certain.

You are to remember that I had not even commenced to treat Mr. Jennings' case. I have not any doubt that I should have cured him perfectly in eighteen months, or possibly it might have extended to two years. Some cases are very rapidly curable, others extremely tedious. Every intelligent physician who will give thought and diligence to the task, will effect a cure.

You know my tract on "The Cardinal Functions of the Brain." I there, by the evidence of innumerable facts, prove, as I think, the high probability of a circulation arterial and venous in its mechanism, through the nerves. Of this system, thus considered, the brain is the heart. The fluid, which is propagated hence through one class of nerves, returns in an altered state through another, and the nature of that fluid is spiritual, though not immaterial, any more than, as I before remarked, light or electricity are so.

By various abuses, among which the habitual use of such agents as green tea is one, this fluid may be affected as to its quality, but it is more frequently disturbed as to equilibrium. This fluid being that which we have in common with spirits, a congestion found upon the masses of brain or nerve, connected with the interior sense, forms a surface unduly exposed, on which disembodied spirits may operate: communication is thus more or less effectually established. Between this brain circulation and the heart circulation there is an intimate sympathy. The seat, or rather the instrument of exterior vision, is the eye. The seat of interior vision is the nervous tissue and brain, immediately about and above the eyebrow. You remember how effectually I dissipated your pictures by the simple application of iced eau-de-cologne. Few cases, however, can be treated exactly alike with anything like rapid success. Cold acts powerfully as a repellant of the nervous fluid. Long enough continued it will even produce that permanent insensibility which we call numbness, and a little longer, muscular as well as sensational paralysis.

I have not, I repeat, the slightest doubt that I should have first dimmed and ultimately sealed that inner eye which Mr. Jennings had inadvertently opened. The same senses are opened in delirium tremens, and entirely shut up again when the overaction of the cerebral heart, and the prodigious nervous congestions that attend it, are terminated by a decided change in the state of the body. It is by acting steadily upon the body, by a simple process, that this result is produced—and inevitably produced—I have never yet failed.

Poor Mr. Jennings made away with himself. But that catastrophe was the result of a totally different malady, which, as it were, projected itself upon the disease which was established. His case was in the distinctive manner a complication, and the complaint under which he really succumbed, was hereditary suicidal mania. Poor Mr. Jennings I cannot call a patient of mine, for I had not even begun to treat his case, and he had not yet given me, I am convinced, his full and unreserved confidence. If the patient do not array himself on the side of the disease, his cure is certain.

Squire Toby's Will

A Ghost Story

Many persons accustomed to travel the old York and London road, in the days of stage-coaches, will remember passing, in the afternoon, say, of an autumn day, in their journey to the capital, about three miles south of the town of Applebury, and a mile and a half before you reach the Old Angel Inn, a large black-and-white house, as those old-fashioned cage-work habitations are termed, dilapidated and weather-stained, with broad lattice windows glimmering all over in the evening sun with little diamond panes, and thrown into relief by a dense background of ancient elms. A wide avenue, now overgrown like a churchyard with grass and weeds, and flanked by double rows of the same dark trees, old and gigantic, with here and there a gap in their solemn files, and sometimes a fallen tree lying across on the avenue, leads up to the halldoor.

Looking up its sombre and lifeless avenue from the top of the London coach, as I have often done, you are struck with so many signs of desertion and decay,—the tufted grass sprouting in the chinks of the steps and window-stones, the smokeless chimneys over which the jackdaws are wheeling, the absence of human life and all its evidence, that you conclude at once that the place is uninhabited and abandoned to decay. The name of this ancient house is Gylingden Hall. Tall hedges and old timber quickly shroud the old place from view, and about a quarter of a mile further on your pass, embowered in melancholy trees, a small and ruinous Saxon chapel, which, time out of mind, has been the burying-place of the family of Marston, and partakes of the neglect and desolation which brood over their ancient dwelling-place.

The grand melancholy of the secluded valley of Gylingden, lonely as an enchanted forest, in which the crows returning to their roosts among the trees, and the straggling deer who peep from beneath their branches, seem to hold a wild and undisturbed dominion, heightens the forlorn aspect of Gylingden Hall.

Of late years repairs have been neglected, and here and there the roof is stripped, and "the stitch in time" has been wanting. At the side of the house exposed to the gales that sweep through the valley like a torrent through its channel, there is not a perfect window left, and the shutters but imperfectly exclude the rain. The ceilings and walls are mildewed and green with damp stains. Here and there, where the drip falls from the ceiling, the floors are rotting. On stormy nights, as the guard described, you can hear the doors clapping in the old house, as far away as old Gryston bridge, and the howl and sobbing of the wind through its empty galleries.

About seventy years ago died the old Squire, Toby Marston, famous in that part of the world for his hounds, his hospitality, and his vices. He had done kind things, and he had fought duels: he had given away money and he had horse-whipped people. He carried with him some blessings and a good many curses, and left behind him an amount of debts and charges upon the estates which appalled his two sons, who had no taste for business or accounts, and had never suspected, till that wicked, openhanded, and swearing old gentleman died, how very nearly he had run the estates into insolvency.

They met at Gylingden Hall. They had the will before them, and lawyers to interpret, and information without stint, as to the encumbrances with which the deceased had saddled them. The will was so framed as to set the two brothers instantly at deadly feud.

These brothers differed in some points; but in one material characteristic they resembled one another, and also their departed father. They never went into a quarrel by halves, and once in, they did not stick at trifles.

The elder, Scroope Marston, the more dangerous man of the two, had never been a favourite of the old Squire. He had no taste for the sports of the field and the pleasures of a rustic life. He was no athlete, and he certainly was not handsome. All this the Squire resented. The young man, who had no respect for him, and outgrew his fear of his violence as he came to manhood, retorted. This aversion, therefore, in the ill-conditioned old man grew into positive hatred. He used to wish that d——d pippin-squeezing, humpbacked rascal Scroope, out of the way of better men—meaning his younger son Charles; and in his cups would talk in a way which even the old and young fellows who followed his hounds, and drank his port, and could stand a reasonable amount of brutality, did not like.

Scroope Marston was slightly deformed, and he had the lean sallow face, piercing black eyes, and black lank hair, which sometimes accompany deformity.

"I'm no feyther o' that hog-backed creature. I'm no sire of hisn, d——n him! I'd as soon call that tongs son o' mine," the old man used to bawl, in allusion to his son's long, lank limbs: "Charlie's a man, but that's a jack-an-ape. He has no good-nature; there's nothing handy, nor manly, nor no one turn of a Marston in him."

And when he was pretty drunk, the old Squire used to swear he should never "sit at the head o' that board; nor frighten away folk from Gylingden Hall wi' his d——d hatchet face—the black loon!"

"Handsome Charlie was the man for his money. He knew what a horse was, and could sit to his bottle; and the lasses were all clean *wad* about him. He was a Marston every inch of his six foot two."

Handsome Charlie and he, however, had also had a row or two. The old Squire was free with his horsewhip as with his tongue, and on occasion when neither weapon was quite practicable, had been known to give a fellow "a tap o' his knuckles." Handsome Charlie, however, thought there was a period at which personal chastisement should cease; and one night, when the port was flowing, there was some allusion to Marion Hayward, the miller's daughter, which for some reason the old gentleman did not like. Being "in liquor," and having clearer ideas about pugilism than self-government, he struck out, to the surprise of all present, at Handsome Charlie. The youth threw back his head scientifically, and nothing followed but the crash of a decanter on the floor. But the old Squire's blood was up, and he bounced from his chair. Up jumped Handsome Charlie, resolved to stand no nonsense. Drunken Squire Lilbourne, intending to mediate, fell flat on the floor, and cut his ear among the glasses. Handsome Charlie caught the thump which the old Squire discharged at him upon his open hand, and catching him by the cravat, swung him with his back to the wall. They said the old man never looked so purple, nor his eyes so goggle before; and then Handsome Charlie pinioned him tight to the wall by both arms.

"Well, I say—come, don't you talk no more nonsense o' that sort, and I won't lick you," croaked the old Squire. "You stopped that un clever, you did. Didn't he? Come, Charlie, man, gie us your hand, I say, and sit down again, lad." And so the battle ended; and I believe it was the last time the Squire raised his hand to Handsome Charlie.

But those days were over. Old Toby Marston lay cold and quiet enough now, under the drip of the mighty ash-tree within the Saxon ruin where so many of the old Marston race returned to dust, and were forgotten. The weather-stained top-boots and leather-breeches, the three-cornered cocked hat to which old gentlemen of that day still clung, and the well-known red waist-coat that reached below his hips, and the fierce pug face of the old Squire, were now but a picture of memory. And the brothers between whom he had planted an irreconcilable quarrel, were now in their new mourning suits, with the gloss still on, debating furiously across the table in the great oak parlour, which had so often resounded to the banter and coarse songs, the oaths and laughter of the congenial neighbours whom the old Squire of Gylingden Hall loved to assemble there.

These young gentlemen, who had grown up in Gylingden Hall, were not accustomed to bridle their tongues, nor, if need be, to hesitate about a blow. Neither had been at the old man's funeral. His death had been sudden. Having been helped to his bed in that hilarious and quarrelsome state which was induced by port and punch, he was found dead in the morning,—his head hanging over the side of the bed, and his face very black and swollen.

Now the Squire's will despoiled his eldest son of Gylingden, which had descended to the heir time out of mind. Scroope Marston was furious. His deep stern voice was heard inveighing against his dead father and living brother, and the heavy thumps on the table with which he enforced his stormy recriminations resounded through the large chamber. Then broke in Charlie's rougher voice, and then came a quick alternation of short sentences, and then both voices together in growing loudness and anger, and at last, swelling the tumult, the expostulations of pacific and frightened lawyers, and at last a sudden break up of the conference. Scroope broke out of the room, his pale furious face showing whiter against his long black hair, his dark fierce eyes blazing, his hands clenched, and looking more ungainly and deformed than ever in the convulsions of his fury.

Very violent words must have passed between them; for Charlie, though he was the winning man, was almost as angry as Scroope. The elder brother was for holding possession of the house, and putting his rival to legal process to oust him. But his legal advisers were clearly against it. So, with a heart boiling over with gall, up he went to London, and found the firm who had managed his father's business fair and communicative enough. They looked into the settlements, and found that Gylingden was excepted. It was very odd, but so it was, specially excepted; so that the right of the old Squire to deal with it by his will could not be questioned.

Notwithstanding all this, Scroope, breathing vengeance and aggression, and quite willing to wreck himself provided he could run his brother down, assailed Handsome Charlie, and battered old Squire Toby's will in the Prerogative Court and also at common law, and the feud between the brothers was knit, and every month their exasperation was heightened.

Scroope was beaten, and defeat did not soften him. Charlie might have forgiven hard words; but he had been himself worsted during the long campaign in some of those skirmishes, special motions. and so forth, that constitute the episodes of a legal epic like that in which the Marston brothers figured as opposing combatants; and the blight of the law-costs had touched him, too, with the usual effect upon the temper of a man of embarrassed means.

Years flew, and brought no healing on their wings. On the contrary, the deep corrosion of this hatred bit deeper by time. Neither brother married. But an accident of a different kind befell the younger, Charles Marston, which abridged his enjoyments very materially.

This was a bad fall from his hunter. There were severe fractures, and there was concussion of the brain. For some time it was thought that he could not recover. He disappointed these evil auguries, however. He did recover, but changed in two essential particulars. He had received an injury to his hip, which doomed him never more to sit in the saddle. And the rollicking animal spirits which hitherto had never failed him, had now taken flight for ever.

He had been for five days in a state of coma—absolute insensibility—and when he recovered consciousness he was haunted by an indescribable anxiety.

Tom Cooper, who had been butler in the palmy days of Gylingden Hall, under old Squire Toby, still maintained his post with old-fashioned fidelity, in these days of faded splendour and frugal housekeeping. Twenty years had passed since the death of his old master. He had grown lean, and stooped, and his face, dark with the peculiar brown of age, furrowed and gnarled, and his temper, except with his master, had waxed surly.

His master had visited Bath and Buxton, and came back, as he went, lame, and halting gloomily about with the aid of a stick. When the hunter was sold, the last tradition of the old life at Gylingden disappeared. The young Squire, as he was still called, excluded by his mischance from the hunting-field, dropped into a solitary way of life, and halted slowly and solitarily about the old place, seldom raising his eyes, and with an appearance of indescribable gloom.

Old Cooper could talk freely on occasion with his master; and one day he said, as he handed him his hat and stick in the hall:

"You should rouse yourself up a bit, Master Charles!"

"It's past rousing with me, old Cooper."

"It's just this, I'm thinking: there's something on your mind, and you won't tell no one. There's no good keeping it on your stomach. You'll be a deal lighter if you tell it. Come, now, what is it, Master Charlie?"

The Squire looked with his round grey eyes straight into Cooper's eyes. He felt that there was a sort of spell broken. It was like the old rule of the ghost who can't speak till it is spoken to. He looked earnestly into old Cooper's face for some seconds, and sighed deeply.

"It ain't the first good guess you've made in your day, old Cooper, and I'm glad you've spoke. It's bin on my mind, sure enough, ever since I had that fall. Come in here after me, and shut the door."

The Squire pushed open the door of the oak parlour, and looked round on the pictures abstractedly. He had not been there for some time, and seating himself on the table, he looked again for a while in Cooper's face before he spoke.

"It's not a great deal, Cooper, but it troubles me, and I would not tell it to the parson nor the doctor; for, God knows what they'd say, though there's nothing to signify in it. But you were always true to the family, and I don't mind if I tell you."

"'Tis as safe with Cooper, Master Charles, as if 'twas locked in a chest, and sunk in a well."

"It's only this," said Charles Marston, looking down on the end of his stick, with which he was tracing lines and circles, "all the time I was lying like dead, as you thought, after that fall, I was with the old master." He raised his eyes to Cooper's again as he spoke, and with an awful oath he repeated—"I was with him, Cooper!"

"He was a good man, sir, in his way," repeated old Cooper, returning his gaze with awe. "He was a good master to me, and a good father to you, and I hope he's happy. May God rest him!"

"Well," said Squire Charles, "it's only this: the whole of that time I was with him, or he was with me—I don't know which.

The upshot is, we were together, and I thought I'd never get out of his hands again, and all the time he was bullying me about some one thing; and if it was to save my life, Tom Cooper, by—— from the time I waked I never could call to mind what it was; and I think I'd give that hand to know; and if you can think of anything it might be—for God's sake! don't be afraid, Tom Cooper, but speak it out, for he threatened me hard, and it was surely him."

Here ensued a silence.

"And what did you think it might be yourself, Master Charles?" said Cooper.

"I han't thought of aught that's likely. I'll never hit on't— *never.* I thought it might happen he knew something about that d—— hump-backed villain, Scroope, that swore before Lawyer Gingham I made away with a paper of settlements—me and father; and, as I hope to be saved, Tom Cooper, there never was a bigger lie! I'd a had the law of him for them identical words, and cast him for more than he's worth; only Lawyer Gingham never goes into nothing for me since money grew scarce in Gylingden; and I can't change my lawyer, I owe him such a hatful of money. But he did, he swore he'd hang me yet for it. He said it in them identical words—he'd never rest till he *hanged* me for it, and I think it was, like enough, something about *that,* the old master was troubled; but it's enough to drive a man mad. I *can't* bring it to mind—I can't remember a word he said, only he threatened awful, and looked—Lord 'a mercy on us!—frightful bad."

"There's no need he should. May the Lord a-mercy on him!" said the old butler.

"No, of course; and you're not to tell a soul, Cooper—not a living soul, mind, that I said he looked bad, nor nothing about it."

"God forbid!" said old Cooper, shaking his head. "But I was thinking, sir, it might ha' been about the slight that's bin so long put on him by having no stone over him, and never a scratch o' a chisel to say who he is."

"Ay! Well, I didn't think o' that. Put on your hat, old Cooper, and come down wi' me; for I'll look after that, at any rate."

There is a bye-path leading by a turnstile to the park, and thence to the picturesque old burying-place, which lies in a nook by the roadside, embowered in ancient trees. It was a fine autumnal sunset, and melancholy lights and long shadows spread their peculiar effects over the landscape as "Handsome Charlie" and the old butler made their way slowly toward the place where Handsome Charlie was himself to lie at last.

"Which of the dogs made that howling all last night?" asked
the Squire, when they had got on a little way.

" 'Twas a strange dog, Master Charlie, in front of the house;
ours was all in the yard—a white dog wi' a black head, he looked
to be, and he was smelling round them mounting-steps the old
master, God be wi' him! set up, the time his knee was bad. When
the tyke got up a' top of them, howlin' up at the windows, I'd a
liked to shy something at him."

"Hullo! Is that like him?" said the Squire, stopping short, and
pointing with his stick at a dirty-white dog, with a large black
head, which was scampering round them in a wide circle, half
crouching with that air of uncertainty and deprecation which dogs
so well know how to assume.

He whistled the dog up. He was a large, half-starved bull-dog.

"That fellow has made a long journey—thin as a whipping-post,
and stained all over, and his claws worn to the stumps," said the
Squire, musingly. "He isn't a bad dog, Cooper. My father liked a
good bull-dog, and knew a cur from a good 'un."

The dog was looking up into the Squire's face with the peculiar
grim visage of his kind, and the Squire was thinking irreverently
how strong a likeness it presented to the character of his father's
fierce pug features when he was clutching his horsewhip and swearing at a keeper.

"If I did right I'd shoot him. He'll worry the cattle, and kill our
dogs," said the Squire. "Hey, Cooper? I'll tell the keeper to look
after him. That fellow could pull down a sheep, and he shan't
live on my mutton."

But the dog was not to be shaken off. He looked wistfully after
the Squire, and after they had got a little way on, he followed
timidly.

It was vain trying to drive him off. The dog ran round them in
wide circles, like the infernal dog in "Faust"; only he left no track
of thin flame behind him. These manoeuvres were executed with
a sort of beseeching air, which flattered and touched the object of
this odd preference. So he called him up again, patted him, and
then and there in a manner adopted him.

The dog now followed their steps dutifully, as if he had belonged to Handsome Charlie all his days. Cooper unlocked the
little iron door, and the dog walked in close behind their heels,
and followed them as they visited the roofless chapel.

The Marstons were lying under the floor of this little building
in rows. There is not a vault. Each has his distinct grave enclosed
in a lining of masonry. Each is surmounted by a stone kist, on the

upper flag of which is enclosed his epitaph, except that of poor old Squire Toby. Over him was nothing but the grass and the line of masonry which indicate the site of the kist, whenever his family should afford him one like the rest.

"Well, it does look shabby. It's the elder brother's business; but if he won't, I'll see to it myself, and I'll take care, old boy, to cut sharp and deep in it, that the elder son having refused to lend a hand the stone was put there by the younger."

They strolled round this little burial ground. The sun was now below the horizon, and the red metallic glow from the clouds, still illuminated by the departed sun, mingled luridity with the twilight. When Charlie peeped again into the little chapel, he saw the ugly dog streched upon Squire Toby's grave, looking at least twice his natural length, and performing such antics as made the young Squire stare. If you have ever seen a cat streched on the floor, with a bunch of Valerian, straining, writhing, rubbing its jaws in long-drawn caresses, and in the absorption of a sensual ecstasy, you have seen a phenomenon resembling that which Handsome Charlie witnessed on looking in.

The head of the brute looked so large, its body long and thin, and its joints so ungainly and dislocated, that the Squire, with old Cooper beside him, looked on with a feeling of disgust and astonishment, which, in a moment or two more, brought the Squire's stick down upon him with a couple of heavy thumps. The beast awakened from his ecstasy, sprang to the head of the grave, and there on a sudden, thick and bandy as before, confronted the Squire, who stood at its foot, with a terrible grin, and eyes that glared with the peculiar green of canine fury.

The next moment the dog was crouching abjectly at the Squire's feet.

"Well, he's a rum 'un!" said old Cooper, looking hard at him.

"I like him," said the Squire.

"I don't," said Cooper.

"But he shan't come in here again," said the Squire.

"I shouldn't wonder if he was a witch," said old Cooper, who remembered more tales of witchcraft than are now current in that part of the world.

"He's a good dog," said the Squire, dreamily. "I remember the time I'd a given a handful for him—but I'll never be good for nothing again. Come along."

And he stooped down and patted him. So up jumped the dog and looked up in his face, as if watching for some sign, ever so slight, which he might obey.

Cooper did not like a bone under that dog's skin. He could not imagine what his master saw to admire in him. He kept him all·night in the gun-room, and the dog accompanied him in his halting rambles about the place. The fonder his master grew of him, the less did Cooper and the other servants like him.

"He hasn't a point of a good dog about him," Cooper would growl. "I think Master Charlie be blind. And old Captain (an old red parrot, who sat chained to a perch in the oak parlour, and conversed with himself, and nibbled at his claws and bit his perch all day),—old Captain, the only living thing, except one or two of us, and the Squire himself, that remembers the old master, the minute he saw the dog, screeched as if he was struck, shakin' his feathers out quite wild, and drops down, poor old soul, a-hangin' by his foot, in a fit."

But there is no accounting for fancies, and the Squire was one of those dogged persons who persist more obstinately in their whims the more they are opposed. But Charles Marston's health suffered by his lameness. The transition from habitual and violent exercise to such a life as his privation now consigned him to, was never made without a risk to health; and a host of dyspeptic annoyances, the existence of which he had never dreamed of before, now beset him in sad earnest. Among these was the now not unfrequent troubling of his sleep with dreams and nightmares. In these his canine favourite invariably had a part and was generally a central, and sometimes a solitary figure. In these visions the dog seemed to stretch himself up the side of the Squire's bed, and in dilated proportions to sit at his feet, with a horrible likeness to the pug features of old Squire Toby, with tricks of wagging his head and throwing up his chin; and then he would talk to him about Scroope, and tell him "all wasn't straight," and that he "must make it up wi' Scroope," that he, the old Squire, had "served him an ill turn," that "time was nigh up," and that "fair was fair,' and he was "troubled where he was, about Scroope."

Then in his dream this semi-human brute would approach his face to his, crawling and crouching up his body, heavy as lead, till the face of the beast was laid on his, with the same odious caresses and stretchings and writhings which he had seen over the old Squire's grave. Then Charlie would wake up with a gasp and a howl, and start upright in the bed, bathed in a cold moisture, and fancy he saw something white sliding off the foot of the bed. Sometimes he thought it might be the curtain with white lining that slipped down, or the coverlet disturbed by his uneasy turnings; but he always fancied, at such moments, that he saw some-

thing white sliding hastily off the bed; and always when he had
been visited by such dreams the dog next morning was more than
usually caressing and servile, as if to obliterate, by a more than
ordinary welcome, the sentiment of disgust which the horror of
the night had left behind it.

The doctor half-satisfied the Squire that there was nothing in
these dreams, which, in one shape or another, invariably attended
forms of indigestion such as he was suffering from.

For a while, as if to corroborate this theory, the dog ceased altogether to figure in them. But at last there came a vision in which,
more unpleasantly than before, he did resume his old place.

In his nightmare the room seemed all but dark; he heard what
he knew to be the dog walking from the door round his bed slowly,
to the side from which he always had come upon it. A portion of
the room was uncarpeted, and he said he distinctly heard the
peculiar tread of a dog, in which the faint clatter of the claws is
audible. It was a light stealthy step, but at every tread the whole
room shook heavily; he felt something place itself at the foot of
his bed, and saw a pair of green eyes staring at him in the dark,
from which he could not remove his own. Then he heard, as he
thought, the old Squire Toby say—"The eleventh hour be passed,
Charlie, and ye've done nothing—you and I 'a done Scroope a
wrong!" and then came a good deal more, and then—"The time's
nigh up, it's going to strike." And with a long low growl, the thing
began to creep up upon his feet; the growl continued, and he
saw the reflection of the up-turned green eyes upon the bed-clothes,
as it began slowly to stretch itself up his body towards his face.
With a loud scream, he waked. The light, which of late the Squire
was accustomed to have in his bed-room, had accidentally gone
out. He was afraid to get up, or even to look about the room for
some time; so sure did he feel of seeing the green eyes in the dark
fixed on him from some corner. He had hardly recovered from his
first agony which nightmare leaves behind it, and was beginning to
collect his thoughts, when he heard the clock strike twelve. And
he bethought him of the words "the eleventh hour be passed—
time's nigh up—it's going to strike!" and he almost feared that he
would hear the voice reopening the subject.

Next morning the Squire came down looking ill.

"Do you know a room, old Cooper," said he, "they used to call
King Herod's Chamber?"

"Ay, sir; the story of King Herod was on the walls o't when I
was a boy."

"There's a closet off it—is there?"

"I can't be sure o' that; but 'tisn't worth your looking at, now; the hangings was rotten, and took off the walls, before you was born; and there's nou't there but some old broken things and lumber. I seed them put there myself by poor Twinks; he was blind of an eye, and footman afterwards. You'll remember Twinks? He died here, about the time o' the great snow. There was a deal o' work to bury him, poor fellow!"

"Get the key, old Cooper; I'll look at the room," said the Squire.

"And what the devil can you want to look at it for?" said Cooper, with the old-world privilege of a rustic butler.

"And what the devil's that to you? But I don't mind if I tell you. I don't want that dog in the gun-room, and I'll put him somewhere else; and I don't care if I put him there."

"A bull-dog in a bedroom! Oons, sir! the folks 'ill say you're clean mad!"

"Well, let them; get you the key, and let us look at the room."

"You'd shoot him if you did right, Master Charlie. You never heard what a noise he kept up all last night in the gun-room, walking to and fro growling like a tiger in a show; and, say what you like, the dog's not worth his feed; he hasn't a point of a dog; he's a bad dog."

"I know a dog better than you—and he's a good dog!" said the Squire, testily.

"If you was a judge of a dog you'd hang that 'un," said Cooper.

"I'm not going to hang him, so there's an end. Go you, and get the key; and don't be talking, mind, when you go down. I may change my mind."

Now this freak of visiting King Herod's room had, in truth, a totally different object from that pretended by the Squire. The voice in his nightmare had uttered a particular direction, which haunted him, and would give him no peace until he had tested it. So far from liking that dog to-day, he was beginning to regard it with a horrible suspicion; and if old Cooper had not stirred his obstinate temper by seeming to dictate, I dare say he would have got rid of that inmate effectually before evening.

Up to the third storey, long disused, he and old Cooper mounted. At the end of a dusty gallery, the room lay. The old tapestry, from which the spacious chamber had taken its name, had long given place to modern paper, and this was mildewed, and in some places hanging from the walls. A thick mantle of dust lay over the floor. Some broken chairs and boards, thick with dust, lay, along with other lumber, piled together at one end of the room.

They entered the closet, which was quite empty. The Squire looked round, and you could hardly have said whether he was relieved or disappointed.

"No furniture here," said the Squire, and looked through the dusty window. "Did you say anything to me lately—I don't mean this morning—about this room, or the closet—or anything—I forget—"

"Lor' bless you! Not I. I han't been thinkin' o' this room this forty year."

"Is there any sort of old furniture called a *buffet*—do you remember?" asked the Squire.

"A buffet? why, yes—to be sure—there was a buffet, sure enough, in this closet, now you bring it to mind," said Cooper. "But it's papered over."

"And what is it?"

"A little cupboard in the wall," answered the old man.

"Ho—I see—and there's such a thing here, is there, under the paper? Show me whereabouts it was."

"Well—I think it was somewhere about here," answered he, rapping his knuckles along the wall opposite the window. "Ay, there it is," he added, as the hollow sound of a wooden door was returned to his knock.

The Squire pulled the loose paper from the wall, and disclosed the doors of a small press, about two feet square, fixed in the wall.

"The very thing for my buckles and pistols, and the rest of my gimcracks," said the Squire. "Come away, we'll leave the dog where he is. Have you the key of that little press?"

No, he had not. The old master had emptied and locked it up, and desired that it should be papered over, and that was the history of it.

Down came the Squire, and took a strong turn-screw from his gun-case; and quietly reascended to King Herod's room, and with little trouble, forced the door of the small press in the closet wall. There were in it some letters and cancelled leases, and also a parchment deed which he took to the window and read with much agitation. It was a supplemental deed executed about a fortnight after the others, and previously to his father's marriage, placing Gylingden under strict settlement to the elder son, in what is called "tail male." Handsome Charlie, in his fraternal litigation, had acquired a smattering of technical knowledge, and he perfectly well knew that the effect of this would be not only to transfer the house and lands to his brother Scroope, but to leave him at the mercy of that exasperated brother, who might recover from him personally every guinea he had ever received by way of rent, from the date of his father's death.

It was a dismal, clouded day, with something threatening in its aspect, and the darkness, where he stood, was made deeper by the top of one of the huge old trees overhanging the window.

In a state of awful confusion he attempted to think over his position. He placed the deed in his pocket, and nearly made up his mind to destroy it. A short time ago he would not have hesitated for a moment under such circumstances; but now his health and his nerves were shattered, and he was under a supernatural alarm which the strange discovery of his deed had powerfully confirmed.

In this state of profound agitation he heard a sniffing at the closet-door, and then an impatient scratch and a long low growl. He screwed his courage up, and, not knowing what to expect, threw the door open and saw the dog, not in his dream-shape, but wriggling with joy, and crouching and fawning with eager submission; and then wandering about the closet, the brute growled awfully into the corners of it, and seemed in an unappeasable agitation.

Then the dog returned and fawned and crouched again at his feet.

After the first moment was over, the sensations of abhorrence and fear began to subside, and he almost reproached himself for requiting the affection of this poor friendless brute with the antipathy which he had really done nothing to earn.

The dog pattered after him down the stairs. Oddly enough, the sight of this animal, after the first revulsion, reassured him; in his eyes, so attached, so good-natured, and palpably so mere a dog.

By the hour of evening the Squire had resolved on a middle course; he would not inform his brother of his discovery, nor yet would he destroy the deed. He would never marry. He was past that time. He would leave a letter, explaining the discovery of the deed, addressed to the only surviving trustee—who had probably forgotten everything about it—and having seen out his own tenure, he would provide that all should be set right after his death. Was not that fair? At all events it quite satisfied what he called his conscience, and he thought it a devilish good compromise for his brother; and he went out, towards sunset, to take his usual walk.

Returning in the darkening twilight, the dog, as usual attending him, began to grow frisky and wild, at first scampering round him in great circles, as before, nearly at the top of his speed, his great head between his paws as he raced. Gradually more excited grew the pace and narrower his circuit, louder and fiercer his continuous growl, and the Squire stopped and grasped his stick hard, for the lurid eyes and grin of the brute threatened an attack. Turning round and round as the excited brute encircled him, and striking vainly at him with his stick, he grew at last so tired that he almost despaired of keeping him longer at bay; when on a sudden the dog stopped short and crawled up to his feet wriggling and crouching submissively.

Nothing could be more apologetic and abject; and when the Squire dealt him two heavy thumps with his stick, the dog whimpered only, and writhed and licked his feet. The Squire sat down on a prostrate tree; and his dumb companion, recovering his wonted spirits immediately, began to sniff and nuzzle among the roots. The Squire felt in his breast-pocket for the deed—it was safe; and again he pondered, in this loneliest of spots, on the question whether he should preserve it for restoration after his death to his brother, or destroy it forthwith. He began rather to lean toward the latter solution, when the long low growl of the dog not far off startled him.

He was sitting in a melancholy grove of old trees, that slants gently westward. Exactly the same odd effect of light I have before described—a faint red glow reflected downward from the upper sky, after the sun had set, now gave to the growing darkness a lurid uncertainty. This grove, which lies in a gentle hollow, owing to its circumscribed horizon on all but one side, has a peculiar character of loneliness.

He got up and peeped over a sort of barrier, accidentally formed of the trunks of felled trees laid one over the other, and saw the dog straining up the other side of it, and hideously stretched out, his ugly head looking in consequence twice the natural size. His dream was coming over him again. And now between the trunks the brute's ungainly head was thrust, and the long neck came straining through, and the body, twining after it like a huge white lizard; and as it came striving and twisting through, it growled and glared as if it would devour him.

As swiftly as his lameness would allow, the Squire hurried from this solitary spot towards the house. What thoughts exactly passed through his mind as he did so, I am sure he could not have told. But when the dog came up with him it seemed appeased, and even in high good humor, and no longer resembled the brute that haunted his dreams.

That night, near ten o'clock, the Squire, a good deal agitated, sent for the keeper, and told him that he believed the dog was mad, and that he must shoot him. He might shoot the dog in the gun-room, where he was—a grain of shot or two in the wainscot did not matter, and the dog must not have a chance of getting out.

The Squire gave the gamekeeper his double-barrelled gun, loaded with heavy shot. He did not go with him beyond the hall. He placed his hand on the keeper's arm; the keeper said his hand trembled, and that he looked "as white as curds."

"Listen a bit!" said the Squire under his breath.

They heard the dog in a state of high excitement in the room—growling ominously, jumping on the window-stool and down again, and running round the room.

"You'll need to be sharp, mind—don't give him a chance—slip in edgeways, d'ye see? and give him both barrels!"

"Not the first mad dog I've knocked over, sir," said the man, looking very serious as he cocked the gun.

As the keeper opened the door, the dog had sprung into the empty grate. He said he "never see sich a stark, staring devil." The beast made a twist round, as if, he thought, to jump up the chimney—"but that wasn't to be done at no price,"—and he made a yell—not like a dog—like a man caught in a mill-crank, and before he could spring, the keeper fired one barrel into him. The dog leaped towards him, and rolled over, receiving the second barrel in his head, as he lay snorting at the keeper's feet!

"I never seed the like; I never heard a screech like that!" said the keeper, recoiling. "It makes a fellow feel queer."

"Quite dead?" asked the Squire.

"Not a stir in him, sir," said the man, pulling him along the floor by the neck.

"Throw him outside the hall-door now," said the Squire; "and mind you pitch him outside the gate to-night—old Cooper says he's a witch," and the pale Squire smiled, "so he shan't lie in Gyl-ingden."

Never was man more relieved than the Squire, and he slept better for a week after this than he had done for many weeks before.

It behooves us all to act promptly on our good resolutions. There is a determined gravitation towards evil, which, if left to itself, will bear down first intentions. If at one moment of superstitious fear, the Squire had made up his mind to a great sacrifice, and resolved in the matter of that deed so strangely recovered, to act honestly by his brother, that resolution very soon gave place to the compromise with fraud, which so conveniently postponed the restitution to the period when further enjoyment on his part was impossible. Then came more tidings of Scroope's violent and minatory language, with always the same burthen—that he would leave no stone unturned to show that there had existed a deed which Charles had either secreted or destroyed, and that he would never rest till he had hanged him.

This of course was wild talk. At first it had only enraged him; but, with his recent guilty knowledge and suppression, had come fear. His danger was the existence of the deed, and little by little he brought himself to a resolution to destroy it. There were many falterings and recoils before he could bring himself to commit this crime. At length, however, he did it, and got rid of the custody of that which at any time might become the instrument of disgrace and ruin. There was relief in this, but also the new and terrible sense of actual guilt.

He had got pretty well rid of his supernatural qualms. It was a different kind of trouble that agitated him now.

But this night, he imagined, he was awakened by a violent shaking of his bed. He could see, in the very imperfect light, two figures at the foot of it, holding each a bed-post. One of these he half-fancied was his brother Scroope, but the other was the old Squire—of that he was sure—and he fancied that they had shaken him up from his sleep. Squire Toby was talking as Charlie wakened, and he heard him say:

"Put out of our own house by you! It won't hold for long. We'll come in together, friendly, and stay. Forewarned, wi' yer eyes open, ye did it; and now Scroope 'll hang you! We'll hang you together! Look at me, you devil's limb."

And the old Squire tremblingly stretched his face, torn with shot and bloody, and growing every moment more and more into the likeness of the dog, and began to stretch himself out and climb the bed over the foot-board, and he saw the figure at the other side, little more than a black shadow, begin also to scale the bed; and there was instantly a dreadful confusion and uproar in the room, and such a grabbling and laughing; he could not catch the words; but, with a scream he woke, and found himself standing on the floor. The phantoms and the clamour were gone, but a crash and ringing of fragments was in his ears. The great china bowl, from which for generations the Marstons of Gylingden had been baptized, had fallen from the mantlepiece, and was smashed on the hearth-stone.

"I've bin dreamin' all night about Mr. Scroope, and I wouldn't

wonder, old Cooper, if he was dead," said the Squire, when he came
down in the morning.

"God forbid! I was adreamed about him, too, sir: I dreamed
he was dammin' and sinkin' about a hole was burnt in his coat,
and the old master, God be wi' him! said—quite plain—I'd 'a
swore 'twas himself—'Cooper, get up, ye d——d land-loupin' thief,
and lend a hand to hang him—for he's a daft cur, and no dog o'
mine.' 'Twas the dog shot over night, I do suppose, as was runnin'
in my old head. I thought old master gied me a punch wi' his
knuckles, and says I, wakenin' up, 'At yer service, sir'; and for a
while I couldn't get it out o' my head, master was in the room
still."

Letters from town soon convinced the Squire that his brother
Scroope, so far from being dead, was particularly active; and
Charlie's attorney wrote to say, in serious alarm, that he had
heard, accidentally, that he intended setting up a case, of a
supplementary deed of settlement, of which he had secondary evidence, which would give him Gylingden. And at this menace Handsome Charlie snapped his fingers, and wrote courageously to his
attorney; abiding what might follow with, however, a secret foreboding.

Scroope threatened loudly now, and swore after his bitter
fashion, and reiterated his old promise of hanging that cheat at
last. In the midst of these menaces and preparations, however, a
sudden peace proclaimed itself: Scroope died, without time even
to make provisions for a posthumous attack upon his brother. It
was one of those cases of disease of the heart in which death is as
sudden as a bullet.

Charlie's exultation was undisguised. It was shocking. Not, of
course, altogether malignant. For there was the expansion consequent on the removal of a secret fear. There was also the comic
piece of luck, that only the day before Scroope had destroyed his
old will, which left to a stranger every farthing he possessed,
intending in a day or two to execute another to the same person,
charged with the express condition of prosecuting the suit against
Charlie.

The result was, that all his possessions went unconditionally
to his brother Charles as his heir. Here were grounds for abun-
dance of savage elation. But there was also the deep-seated hatred
of half a life of mutual and persistent aggression and revilings;
and Handsome Charlie was capable of nursing a grudge, and enjoying a revenge with his whole heart.

He would gladly have prevented his brother's being buried in the old Gylingden chapel, where he wished to lie; but his lawyers doubted his power, and he was not quite proof against the scandal which would attend his turning back the funeral, which would, he knew, be attended by some of the country gentry and others, with an hereditary regard for the Marstons.

But he warned his servants that not one of them were to attend it; promising, with oaths and curses not to be disregarded, that any one of them who did so, should find the door shut in his face on his return.

I don't think, with the exception of old Cooper, that the servants cared for this prohibition, except as it baulked a curiosity always strong in the solitude of the country. Cooper was very much vexed that the eldest son of the old Squire should be buried in the old family chapel, and no sign of decent respect from Gylingden Hall. He asked his master, whether he would not, at least, have some wine and refreshments in the oak parlour, in case any of the country gentlemen who paid this respect to the old family should come up to the house? But the Squire only swore at him, told him to mind his own business, and ordered him to say, if such a thing happened, that he was out, and no preparations made, and, in fact, to send them away as they came. Cooper expostulated stoutly, and the Squire grew angrier; and after a tempestuous scene, took his hat and stick and walked out, just as the funeral descending the valley from the direction of the "Old Angel Inn" came in sight.

Old Cooper prowled about disconsolately, and counted the carriages as well as he could from the gate. When the funeral was over, and they began to drive away, he returned to the hall, the door of which lay open, and as usual deserted. Before he reached it quite, a mourning coach drove up, and two gentlemen in black cloaks, and crapes to their hats, got out, and without looking to the right or the left, went up the steps into the house. Cooper followed them slowly. The carriage had, he supposed, gone round to the yard, for, when he reached the door, it was no longer there.

So he followed the two mourners into the house. In the hall he found a fellow-servant, who said he had seen two gentlemen, in black cloaks, pass through the hall, and go up the stairs without removing their hats, or asking leave of anyone. This was very odd, old Cooper thought, and a great liberty; so upstairs he went to make them out.

But he could not find them then, nor ever. And from that hour the house was troubled.

In a little time there was not one of the servants who had not something to tell. Steps and voices followed them sometimes in the passages, and tittering whispers, always minatory, scared them at corners of the galleries, or from dark recesses; so that they would return panic-stricken to be rebuked by thin Mrs. Beckett, who looked on such stories as worse than idle. But Mrs. Beckett herself, a short time after, took a very different view of the matter.

She had herself begun to hear these voices, and with this formidable aggravation, that they came always when she was at her prayers, which she had been punctual in saying all her life, and utterly interrupted them. She was scared at such moments by dropping words and sentences, which grew, as she persisted, into threats and blasphemies.

These voices were not always in the room. They called, as she fancied, through the walls, very thick in that old house, from the neighbouring apartments, sometimes on one side, sometimes on the other; sometimes they seemed to holloa from distant lobbies, and came muffled, but threateningly, through the long panelled passages. As they approached they grew furious, as if several voices were speaking together. Whenever, as I said, this worthy woman applied herself to her devotions, these horrible sentences came hurrying towards the door, and, in panic, she would start from her knees, and all then would subside except the thumping of her heart against her stays, and the dreadful tremors of her nerves.

What these voices said, Mrs. Beckett never could quite remember one minute after they had ceased speaking; one sentence chased another away; gibe and menace and impious denunciation, each hideously articulate, were lost as soon as heard. And this added to the effect of these terrifying mockeries and invectives, that she could not, by any effort, retain their exact import, although their horrible character remained vividly present in her mind.

For a long time the Squire seemed to be the only person in the house absolutely unconscious of these annoyances. Mrs. Beckett had twice made up her mind within the week to leave. A prudent woman, however, who has been comfortable for more than twenty years in a place, thinks oftener than twice before she leaves it. She and old Cooper were the only servants in the house who remembered the good old housekeeping in Squire Toby's day. The others were few, and such as could hardly be accounted regular servants. Meg Dobbs, who acted as housemaid, would not sleep in the house, but walked home in trepidation, to her father's, at the gatehouse, under the escort of her little brother, every night. Old Mrs. Beckett, who was high and mighty with the make-shift servants of

808.83
L52g

fallen Gylingden, let herself down all at once, and made Mrs.
Kymes and the kitchen-maid move their beds into her large and
faded room, and there, very frankly, shared her nightly terrors
with them.

Old Cooper was testy and captious about these stories. He was
already uncomfortable enough by reason of the entrance of the
two muffled figures into the house, about which there could be
no mistake. His own eyes had seen them. He refused to credit the
stories of the women, and affected to think that the two mourners
might have left the house and driven away, on finding no one to
receive them.

Old Cooper was summoned at night to the oak parlour, where
the Squire was smoking.

"I say, Cooper," said the Squire, looking pale and angry, "what
for ha' you been frightenin' they crazy women wi' your plaguy
stories? d—— me, if you see ghosts here it's no place for you, and
it's time you should pack. I won't be left without servants. Here
has been old Beckett wi' the cook and the kitchenmaid, as white
as pipe clay, all in a row, to tell me I must have a parson to sleep
among them, and preach down the devil! Upon my soul, you're a
wise old body, filling their heads wi' maggots! and Meg goes down
to the lodge every night, afeared to lie in the house—all your doing, wi' your old wives stories,—ye withered old Tom o' Bedlam!"

"I'm not to blame, Master Charles. 'Tisn't along o' no stories o'
mine, for I'm never done telling 'em it's all vanity and vapours.
Mrs. Beckett 'ill tell you that, and there's been many a wry word
betwixt us on the head o't. Whate'er I may *think*," said old Cooper,
significantly, and looking askance, with the sternness of fear in
the Squire's face.

The Squire averted his eyes, and muttered angrily to himself,
and turned away to knock the ashes out of his pipe on the hob,
and then turning suddenly round upon Cooper again, he spoke,
with a pale face, but not quite so angrily as before.

"I know you're no fool, old Cooper, when you like. Suppose
there was such a thing as a ghost here, don't you see, it ain't to
them snipe-headed women it 'id go to tell its story. What ails you,
man, that you should think ought about it, but just what *I* think?
You had a good headpiece o' yer own once, Cooper, don't be you
clappin' a goosecap over it, as my poor father used to say; d—— it,
old boy, you mustn't let 'em be fools, settin' one another wild wi'
their blether, and makin' the folks talk what they shouldn't, about
Gylingden and the family. I don't think ye'd like that, old Cooper,
I'm sure ye wouldn't. The women has gone out o' the kitchen,

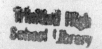
Winsted High
School Library

27,446

make up a bit o' fire, and get your pipe. I'll go to you, when I finish this one, and we'll smoke a bit together, and a glass o' brandy and water."

Down went the old butler, not altogether unused to such condescensions in that disorderly and lonely household; and let not those who can choose their company, be too hard on the Squire who couldn't.

When he got things tidy, as he said, he sat down in that big old kitchen, with his feet on the fender, the kitchen candle burning in a great brass candlestick, which stood on the deal table at his elbow, with the brandy bottle and tumblers beside it, and Cooper's pipe also in readiness. And these preparations completed, the old butler, who had remembered other generations and better times, fell into rumination, and so, gradually, into a deep sleep.

Old Cooper was half awakened by some one laughing low, near his head. He was dreaming of old times in the Hall, and fancied one of "the young gentlemen" going to play him a trick, and he mumbled something in his sleep, from which he was awakened by a stern deep voice, saying, "You wern't at the funeral; I might take your life, I'll take your ear." At the same moment, the side of his head received a violent push, and he started to his feet. The fire had gone down, and he was chilled. The candle was expiring in the socket, and threw on the white wall long shadows, that danced up and down from the ceiling to the ground, and their black outlines he fancied resembled the two men in cloaks, whom he remembered with a profound horror.

He took the candle, with all the haste he could, getting along the passage, on whose walls the same dance of black shadows was continued, very anxious to reach his room before the light should go out. He was startled half out of his wits by the sudden clang of his master's bell, close over his head, ringing furiously.

"Ha, ha! There it goes—yes, sure enough," said Cooper, reassuring himself with the sound of his own voice, as he hastened on, hearing more and more distinct every moment the same furious ringing. "He's fell asleep, like me; that's it, and his lights is out, I lay you fifty—"

When he turned the handle of the door of the oak parlour, the Squire wildly called, "Who's *there?*" in the tone of a man who expects a robber.

"It's me, old Cooper, all right, Master Charlie, you didn't come to the kitchen after all, sir."

"I'm very bad, Cooper; I don't know how I've been. Did you meet anything?" asked the Squire.

"No," said Cooper.

They stared on one another.

"Come here—stay here! Don't you leave me! Look round the room, and say is all right; and gie us your hand, old Cooper, for I must hold it." The Squire's was damp and cold, and trembled very much. It was not very far from day-break now.

After a time he spoke again: "I 'a done many a thing I shouldn't; I'm not fit to go, and wi' God's blessin' I'll look to it— why shouldn't I? I'm as lame as old Billy—I'll never be able to do any good no more, and I'll give over drinking, and marry, as I ought to 'a done long ago—none o' yer fine ladies, but a good homely wench; there's Farmer Crump's youngest daughter, a good lass, and discreet. What for shouldn't I take her? She'd take care o' me and wouldn't bring a head full o' romances here, and man-tua-makers' trumpery, and I'll talk with the parson, and I'll do what's fair wi' everyone; and mind, I said I'm sorry for many a thing I 'a done."

A wild cold dawn had by this time broken. The Squire, Cooper said, looked "awful bad," as he got his hat and stick, and sallied out for a walk, instead of going to his bed, as Cooper besought him, looking so wild and distracted, that it was plain his object was simply to escape from the house. It was twelve o'clock when the Squire walked into the kitchen, where he was sure of finding some of the servants, looking as if ten years had passed over him since yesterday. He pulled a stool by the fire, without speaking a word, and sat down. Cooper had sent to Applebury for the doc-tor, who had just arrived, but the Squire would not go to him. "If he wants to see me, he may come here," he muttered as often as Cooper urged him. So the doctor did come, charily enough, and found the Squire very much worse than he had expected.

The Squire resisted the order to get to his bed. But the doctor insisted under a threat of death, at which his patient quailed.

"Well, I'll do what you say—only this—you must let old Cooper and Dick Keeper stay wi' me. I mustn't be left alone, and they must keep awake o' nights; and stay a while, do *you*. When I get round a bit, I'll go and live in a town. It's dull livin' here, now that I can't do nou't as I used, and I'll live a better life, mind ye; ye heard me say that, and I don't care who laughs, and I'll talk wi' the parson. I like 'em to laugh, hang 'em, it's a sign I'm doin' right, at last."

The doctor sent a couple of nurses from the County Hospital, not choosing to trust his patient to the management he had se-lected, and he went down himself to Gylingden to meet them in the evening. Old Cooper was ordered to occupy the dressing-room, and sit up at night, which satisfied the Squire, who was in a strangely excited state, very low, and threatened, the doctor said, with fever.

The clergyman came, an old, gentle, "book-learned" man, and talked and prayed with him late that evening. After he had gone the Squire called the nurses to his bedside, and said:

"There's a fellow sometimes comes; you'll never mind him. He looks in at the door and beckons,—a thin, hump-backed chap in mourning, wi' black gloves on; ye'll know him by his lean face, as brown as the wainscot: don't ye mind his smilin'. You don't go out to him, nor ask him in; he won't say nout; and if he grows anger'd and looks awry at ye, don't ye be afeared, for he can't hurt ye, and he'll grow tired waitin', and go away; and for God's sake mind ye don't ask him in, nor go out after him!"

The nurses put their heads together when this was over, and held afterwards a whispering conference with old Cooper. "Law bless ye!—no, there's no madman in the house," he protested; "not a soul but what ye saw,—it's just a trifle o' the fever in his head—no more."

The Squire grew worse as the night wore on. He was heavy and delirious, talking of all sorts of things—of wine, and dogs, and lawyers; and then he began to talk, as it were, to his brother Scroope. As he did so, Mrs. Oliver, the nurse, who was sitting up alone with him, heard, as she thought, a hand softly laid on the door-handle outside, and a stealthy attempt to turn it. "Lord bless us! who's there?" she cried, and her heart jumped into her mouth, as she thought of the hump-backed man in black, who was to put in his head smiling and beckoning—"Mr. Cooper! sir! are you there?" she cried. "Come here, Mr. Cooper, please—do, sir, quick!"

Old Cooper, called up from his doze by the fire, stumbled in from the dressing-room, and Mrs. Oliver seized him tightly as he emerged.

"The man with the hump has been atryin' the door, Mr. Cooper, as sure as I am here." The Squire was moaning and mumbling in his fever, understanding nothing, as she spoke. "No, no! Mrs. Oliver, ma'am, it's impossible, for there's no sich man in the house: what is Master Charlie sayin'?"

"He's saying *Scroope* every minute, whatever he means by that, and—and—hisht!—listen—there's the handle again," and, with a loud scream, she added—"Look at his head and neck in at the door!" and in her tremour she strained old Cooper in an agonizing embrace.

The candle was flaring, and there was a wavering shadow at the door that looked like the head of a man with a long neck, and a longish sharp nose, peeping in and drawing back.

"Don't be a d—— fool, ma'am!" cried Cooper, very white, and shaking her with all his might. "It's only the candle, I tell you— nothing in life but that. Don't you see?" and he raised the light; "and I'm sure there was no one at the door, and I'll try, if you let me go."

The other nurse was asleep on the sofa, and Mrs. Oliver called her up in a panic, for company, as old Cooper opened the door. There was no one near it, but at the angle of the gallery was a shadow resembling that which he had seen in the room. He raised the candle a little, and it seemed to beckon with a long hand as the head drew back. "Shadow from the candle!" exclaimed Cooper aloud, resolved not to yield to Mrs. Oliver's panic; and, candle in hand, he walked to the corner. There was nothing. He could not forbear peeping down the long gallery from this point, and as he moved the light, he saw precisely the same sort of shadow, a little further down, and as he advanced the same withdrawal, and beckon. "Gammon!" said he; "it is nout but the candle." And on he went, growing half angry and half frightened at the persistency with which this ugly shadow—a literal shadow he was sure it was—presented itself. As he drew near the point where it now appeared, it seemed to collect itself, and nearly dissolve in the central panel of an old carved cabinet which he was now approaching.

In the centre panel of this is a sort of boss carved into a wolf's head. The light fell oddly upon this, and the fugitive shadow seemed to be breaking up, and re-arranging itself as oddly. The eye-ball gleamed with a point of reflected light, which glittered also upon the grinning mouth, and he saw the long, sharp nose of Scroope Marston, and his fierce eye looking at him, he thought, with a steadfast meaning.

Old Cooper stood gazing upon this sight, unable to move, till he saw the face, and the figure that belonged to it, begin gradually to emerge from the wood. At the same time he heard voices approaching rapidly up a side gallery, and Cooper, with a loud "Lord a-mercy on us!" turned and ran back again, pursued by a sound that seemed to shake the old house like a mighty gust of wind.

Into his master's room burst old Cooper, half wild with fear, and clapped the door and turned the key in a twinkling, looking as if he had been pursued by murderers.

"Did you hear it?" whispered Cooper, now standing near the dressing-room door. They all listened, but not a sound from without disturbed the utter stillness of night. "God bless us! I doubt it's my old head that's gone crazy!" exclaimed Cooper.

He would tell them nothing but that he was himself "an old fool," to be frightened by their talk, and that "the rattle of a window, or the dropping o' a pin" was enough to scare him now; and so he helped himself through the night with brandy, and sat up talking by his master's fire.

The Squire recovered slowly from his brain fever, but not perfectly. A very little thing, the doctor said, would suffice to upset him. He was not yet sufficiently strong to remove for change of scene and air, which were necessary for his complete restoration.

Cooper slept in the dressing-room, and was now his only nightly attendant. The ways of the invalid were odd: he liked, half sitting up in his bed, to smoke his churchwarden o' nights, and made old Cooper smoke, for company, at the fire-side. As the Squire and his humble friend indulged in it, smoking is a taciturn pleasure, and it was not until the Master of Gylingden had finished his third pipe that he essayed conversation, and when he did, the subject was not such as Cooper would have chosen.

"I say, old Cooper, look in my face, and don't be afeared to speak out," said the Squire, looking at him with a steady, cunning smile; "you know all this time, as well as I do, who's in the house. You needn't deny—hey?—Scroope and my father?"

"Don't you be talking like that, Charlie," said old Cooper, rather sternly and frightened, after a long silence; still looking in his face, which did not change.

"What's the good of shammin', Cooper? Scroope's took the hearin' o' yer right ear—you know he did. He's looking angry. He's nigh took my life wi' this fever. But he's not done wi' me yet, and he looks awful wicked. Ye saw him—ye know ye did."

Cooper was awfully frightened, and the odd smile on the Squire's lips frightened him still more. He dropped his pipe, and stood gazing in silence at his master, and feeling as if he were in a dream.

"If ye think so, ye should not be smiling like that," said Cooper, grimly.

"I'm tired, Cooper, and it's as well to smile as t'other thing; so I'll even smile while I can. You know what they mean to do wi' me. That's all I wanted to say. Now, lad, go on wi' yer pipe—I'm goin' asleep."

So the Squire turned over in his bed, and lay down serenely, with his head on the pillow. Old Cooper looked at him, and glanced at the door, and then half-filled his tumbler with brandy, and drank it off, and felt better, and got to his bed in the dressing-room.

In the dead of night he was suddenly awakened by the Squire, who was standing, in his dressing-gown and slippers, by his bed.

"I've brought you a bit o' a present. I got the rents o' Hazelden yesterday, and ye'll keep that for yourself—it's a fifty—and give t'other to Nelly Carwell to-morrow; I'll sleep the sounder; and I saw Scroope since; he's not such a bad 'un after all, old fellow! He's got a crape over his face—for I told him I couldn't bear it; and I'd do many a thing for him now. I never could stand shilly-shally. Good-night, old Cooper!"

And the Squire laid his trembling hand kindly on the old man's shoulder, and returned to his own room.

"I don't half like how he is. Doctor don't come half often enough. I don't like that queer smile o' his, and his hand was as cold as death. I hope in God his brain's not a-turnin'!" With these reflections, Cooper turned to the pleasanter subject of his present, and at last fell asleep.

In the morning, when he went into the Squire's room, the Squire had left his bed. "Never mind; he'll come back, like a bad shillin'," thought old Cooper, preparing the room as usual. But he did not return. Then began an uneasiness, succeeded by a panic, when it began to be plain that the Squire was not in the house. What had become of him? None of his clothes, but his dressing-gown and slippers were missing. Had he left the house, in his present sickly state, in that garb? and, if so, could he be in his right senses; and was there a chance of his surviving a cold, damp night, so passed, in the open air?

Tom Edwards was up to the house, and told them, that, walking a mile or so that morning, at four o'clock—there being no moon—along with Farmer Nokes, who was driving his cart to market, in the dark, three men walked, in front of the horse, not twenty yards before them, all the way from near Gylingden Lodge to the burial ground, the gate of which was opened for them from within, and the three men entered, and the gate was shut. Tom Edwards thought they were gone in to make preparations for a funeral of some member of the Marston family. But the occurrence seemed to Cooper, who knew there was no such thing, horribly ominous.

He now commenced a careful search, and at last bethought him of the lonely upper storey, and King Herod's chamber. He

saw nothing changed there, but the closet door was shut, and, dark
as was the morning, something, like a large white knot sticking
out over the door, caught his eye.

The door resisted his efforts to open it for a time; some great
weight forced it down against the floor; at length, however, it did
yield a little, and a heavy crash, shaking the whole floor, and sending an echo flying through all the silent corridors, with a sound
like receding laughter, half stunned him.

When he pushed open the door, his master was lying dead upon
the floor. His cravat was drawn halter-wise tight round his throat,
and had done its work well. The body was cold, and had been
long dead.

In due course the coroner held his inquest, and the jury pronounced, "that the deceased, Charles Marston, had died by his
own hand, in a state of temporary insanity." But old Cooper had
his own opinion about the Squire's death, though his lips were
sealed, and he never spoke about it. He went and lived for the resi-
due of his days in York, where there are still people who remember him, a taciturn and surly old man, who attended church regularly, and also drank a little, and was known to have saved some
money.

The Fortunes of
Sir Robert Ardagh

*Being a Second Extract from the Papers of
the Late Father Purcell*

The earth hath bubbles as the water hath—.
And these are of them.

In the south of Ireland, and on the borders of the county of
Limerick, there lies a district of two or three miles in length, which
is rendered interesting by the fact that it is one of the very few
spots throughout this country, in which some fragments of abor-
iginal wood have found a refuge. It has little or none of the lordly
character of the American forests; for the axe has felled its oldest
and its grandest trees; but in the close wood which survives, live
all the wild and pleasing peculiarities of nature—its complete
irregularity—its vistas, in whose perspective the quiet cattle are
peacefully browsing—its refreshing glades, where the grey rocks
arise from amid the nodding fern—the silvery shafts of the old
birch trees—the knotted trunks of the hoary oak—the grotesque
but graceful branches, which never shed their honours under the
tyrant pruning hook— the soft green sward—the chequered light
and shade—the wild luxuriant weeds—its lichen and its moss—all,
all are beautiful alike in the green freshness of spring, or in the
sadness and sear of autumn—their beauty is of that kind which
makes the heart full with joy—appealing to the affections with a
power which belongs to nature only. This wood runs up, from
below the base, to the ridge of a long line of irregular hills, having
perhaps in primitive times, formed but the skirting of some mighty
forest which occupied the level below.

But now, alas, whither have we drifted?—whither has the tide of
civilization borne us?—it has passed over a land unprepared for it
—it has left nakedness behind it—we have lost our forests, but our

marauders remain—we have destroyed all that is picturesque, while we have retained everything that is revolting in barbarism. Through the midst of this woodland, there runs a deep gulley or glen; where the stillness of the scene is broken in upon by the brawling of a mountain stream, which, however, in the winter season, swells into a rapid and formidable torrent.

There is one point at which the glen becomes extremely deep and narrow, the sides descend to the depth of some hundred feet, and are so steep as to be nearly perpendicular. The wild trees which have taken root in the crannies and chasms of the rock, have so intersected and entangled, that one can with difficulty catch a glimpse of the stream, which wheels, flashes, and foams below, as if exulting in the surrounding silence and solitude.

This spot was not unwisely chosen, as a point of no ordinary strength, for the erection of a massive square tower or keep, one side of which rises as if in continuation of the precipitous cliff on which it is based. Originally, the only mode of ingress was by a narrow portal, in the very wall which overtopped the precipice; opening upon a ledge of rock which afforded a precarious pathway, cautiously intersected, however, by a deep trench cut with great labour in the living rock; so that, in its original state, and before the introduction of artillery into the art of war, this tower might have been pronounced, and that not presumptuously, almost impregnable.

The progress of improvement, and the increasing security of the times had, however, tempted its successive proprietors, if not to adorn, at least to enlarge their premises, and at about the middle of the last century, when the castle was last inhabited, the original square tower formed but a small part of the edifice.

The castle, and a wide tract of the surrounding country had from time immemorial, belonged to a family, which, for distinctness, we shall call by the name of Ardagh; and, owing to the associations which, in Ireland, almost always attach to scenes which have long witnessed alike, the exercise of stern feudal authority, and of that savage hospitality which distinguished the good old times, this building has become the subject and the scene of many wild and extraordinary traditions. One of them I have been enabled, by a personal acquaintance with an eye-witness of the events, to trace to its origin; and yet it is hard to say, whether the events which I am about to record, appear more strange or improbable, as seen through the distorting medium of tradition, or in the appalling dimness of uncertainty, which surrounds the reality.

Tradition says that, sometime in the last century, Sir Robert

Ardagh, a young man, and the last heir of that family, went abroad and served in foreign armies, and that having acquired considerable honour and emolument, he settled at Castle Ardagh, the building we have just now attempted to describe. He was what the country people call a *dark* man; that is, he was considered morose, reserved, and ill-tempered; and as it was supposed from the utter solitude of his life, was upon no terms of cordiality with the other members of his family.

The only occasion upon which he broke through the solitary monotony of his life, was during the continuance of the racing season, and immediately subsequent to it; at which time he was to be seen among the busiest upon the course, betting deeply and unhesitatingly, and invariably with success. Sir Robert was, however, too well-known as a man of honour, and of too high a family to be suspected of any unfair dealing. He was, moreover, a soldier, and a man of an intrepid as well as of a haughty character, and no one cared to hazard a surmise, the consequences of which would be felt most probably by its originator only. Gossip, however, was not silent—it was remarked that Sir Robert never appeared at the race ground, which was the only place of public resort which he frequented, except in company with a certain strange looking person, who was never seen elsewhere, or under other circumstances. It was remarked, too, that this man, whose relation to Sir Robert was never distinctly ascertained, was the only person to whom he seemed to speak unnecessarily; it was observed, that while with the country gentry he exchanged no further communication than what was unavoidable in arranging his sporting transactions, with this person he would converse earnestly and frequently. Tradition asserts, that to enhance the curiosity which this unaccountable and exclusive preference excited, the stranger possessed some striking and unpleasant peculiarities of person and of garb—she does not say, however, what these were—but they, in conjunction with Sir Robert's secluded habits, and extraordinary run of luck—a success which was supposed to result from the suggestions and immediate advice of the unknown—were sufficient to warrant report in pronouncing that there was something *queer* in the wind, and in surmising that Sir Robert was playing a fearful and a hazardous game, and that in short, his strange companion was little better than the devil himself.

Years, however, rolled quietly away, and nothing novel occurred in the arrangements of Castle Ardagh, excepting that Sir Robert parted with his odd companion, but as nobody could tell whence he came, so nobody could say whither he had gone. Sir Robert's habits, however, underwent no consequent change; he continued regularly to frequent the race meetings, without mixing at all in the convivialities of the gentry, and immediately afterwards to relapse into the secluded monotony of his ordinary life.

It was said that he had accumulated vast sums of money—and, as his bets were always successful, and always large, such must have been the case. He did not suffer the acquisition of wealth, however, to influence his hospitality or his housekeeping—he neither purchased land, nor extended his establishment; and his mode of enjoying his money must have been altogether that of the miser—consisting, merely, in the pleasure of touching and telling his gold, and in the consciousness of wealth. Sir Robert's temper, so far from improving, became more than ever gloomy and morose. He sometimes carried the indulgence of his evil dispositions to such a height, that it bordered upon insanity. During these paroxysms, he would neither eat, drink, nor sleep. On such occasions he insisted on perfect privacy, even from the intrusion of his most trusted servants;—his voice was frequently heard, sometimes in earnest supplication, sometimes raised as if in loud and angry altercation, with some unknown visitant—sometimes he would, for hours together, walk to and fro, throughout the long oak wainscotted apartment, which he generally occupied, with wild gesticulations and agitated pace, in the manner of one who has been roused to a state of unnatural excitement, by some sudden and appalling intimation.

These paroxysms of apparent lunacy were so frightful, that during their continuance, even his oldest and most faithful domestics dared not approach him; consequently, his hours of agony were never intruded upon, and the mysterious causes of his sufferings appeared likely to remain hidden for ever. On one occasion, a fit of this kind continued for an unusual time—the ordinary term of their duration, about two days, had been long past—and the old servant, who generally waited upon Sir Robert, after these visitations, having in vain listened for the well-known tinkle of his master's hand-bell, began to feel extremely anxious; he feared that his master might have died from sheer exhaustion, or perhaps put an end to his own existence, during his miserable depression. These fears at length became so strong, that having in vain urged some of his brother-servants to accompany him, he determined to go up alone, and himself see whether any accident had befallen Sir Robert. He traversed the several passages which conducted from the new to the more ancient parts of the mansion; and having arrived in the old hall of the castle, the utter silence of the hour, for it was very late in the night, the idea of the nature of the enterprise in which he was engaging himself, a sensation of remoteness from anything like human companionship, but more than all the vivid but undefined anticipation of something horrible, came upon him with such oppressive weight, that he hesitated as to whither he should proceed. Real uneasiness, however, respecting the fate of his master, for whom he felt that kind of attachment, which the force of habitual intercourse, not unfrequently engenders respecting objects not in themselves amiable —and also a latent unwillingness to expose his weakness to the ridicule of his fellow-servants, combined to overcome his reluctance; and he had just placed his foot upon the first step of the staircase, which conducted to his master's chamber, when his attention was arrested by a low but distinct knocking at the hall-door. Not, perhaps, very sorry at finding thus an excuse even for deferring his intended expedition, he placed the candle upon a stone block which lay in the hall, and approached the door, uncertain whether his ears had not deceived him. This doubt was justified by the circumstance, that the hall entrance had been for nearly fifty years disused as a mode of ingress to the castle. The situation of this gate also, which we have endeavoured to describe, opening upon a narrow ledge of rock which overhangs a perilous cliff, rendered it at all times, but particularly at night, a dangerous entrance; this shelving platform of rock, which formed the only avenue to the door, was divided, as I have already stated, by a broad chasm, the planks across which had long disappeared by decay or otherwise, so that it seemed at least highly improbable that any man could have found his way across the passage in safety to the door—more particularly, on a night like that, of singular darkness. The old man, therefore, listened attentively, to ascertain whether the first application should be followed by another; he had not long to wait; the same low but singularly distinct knocking was repeated; so low that it seemed as if the applicant had employed no harder or heavier instrument than his hand, and yet despite the immense thickness of the door, so very distinct, that he could not mistake the sound. It was repeated a third time, without any increase of loudness; and the old man obeying an impulse for which to his dying hour, he could never account, proceeded to remove, one by one, the three great oaken bars which secured the door. Time and damp had effectually corroded the iron chambers of the lock, so that it afforded little resistance. With some effort, as he believed, assisted from without, the old servant succeeded in opening the door; and a low, square-built

figure, apparently that of a man wrapped in a large black cloak,
entered the hall. The servant could not see much of this visitant
with any distinctness; his dress appeared foreign, the skirt of his
ample cloak was thrown over one shoulder; he wore a large felt
hat, with a very heavy leaf, from under which escaped what appeared to be a mass of long sooty-black hair;—his feet were cased
in heavy ridingboots. Such were the few particulars which the
servant had time and light to observe. The stranger desired him
to let his master know instantly that a friend had come, by appointment, to settle some business with him. The servant hesitated,
but a slight motion on the part of his visitor, as if to possess himself
of the candle, determined him; so taking it in his hand, he ascended
the castle stairs, leaving his guest in the hall.

On reaching the apartment which opened upon the oak-cham-
ber, he was surprised to observe the door of that room partly open,
and the room itself lit up. He paused, but there was no sound—
he looked in, and saw Sir Robert—his head, and the upper part of
his body, reclining on a table, upon which burned a lamp; his arms
were stretched forward on either side, and perfectly motionless; it
appeared that having been sitting at the table, he had thus sunk
forward, either dead or in a swoon. There was no sound of breathing; all was silent, except the sharp ticking of a watch, which lay
beside the lamp. The servant coughed twice or thrice, but with no
effect—his fears now almost amounted to certainty, and he was
approaching the table on which his master partly lay—to satisfy
himself of his death—when Sir Robert slowly raised his head, and
throwing himself back in his chair, fixed his eyes in a ghastly and
uncertain gaze upon his attendant. At length he said, slowly and
painfully, as if he dreaded the answer—

"In God's name, what are you?"

"Sir," said the servant, "a strange gentleman wants to see you
below."

At this intimation, Sir Robert, starting on his legs, and tossing
his arms wildly upwards, uttered a shriek of such appalling and
despairing terror, that it was almost too fearful for human endur-
ance; and long after the sound had ceased, it seemed to the terrified
imagination of the old servant, to roll through the deserted passages in bursts of unnatural laughter. After a few moments, Sir
Robert said—

"Can't you send him away? Why does he come so soon? Oh God!
oh God! let him leave me for an hour—a little time. I can't see him
now—try to get him away. You see I can't go down now—I have
not strength. Oh God! oh God! let him come back in an hour—it is

not long to wait. He cannot lose any thing by it—nothing, nothing, nothing. Tell him that—say any thing to him."

The servant went down. In his own words, he did not feel the stairs under him, till he got to the hall. The figure stood exactly as he had left it. He delivered his master's message as coherently as he could. The stranger replied in a careless tone—

"If Sir Robert will not come down to me, I must go up to him."

The man returned, and to his surprise he found his master much more composed in manner. He listened to the message; and though the cold perspiration stood in drops upon his forehead, faster than he could wipe it away, his manner had lost the dreadful agitation which had marked it before. He rose feebly, and casting a last look of agony behind him, passed from the room to the lobby, where he signed to his attendant not to follow him. The man moved as far as the head of the staircase, from whence he had a tolerably distinct view of the hall, which was imperfectly lighted by the candle he had left there.

He saw his master reel, rather than walk down the stairs, clinging all the way to the banisters. He walked on as if about to sink every moment from weakness. The figure advanced as if to meet him, and in passing struck down the light. The servant could see no more; but there was a sound of struggling, renewed at intervals with silent but fearful energy. It was evident, however, that the parties were approaching the door, for he heard the solid oak sound twice or thrice, as the feet of the combatants, in shuffling hither and thither over the floor, struck upon it. After a slight pause he heard the door thrown open, with such violence that the leaf struck the sidewall of the hall, and it was so dark without that this was made known in no other way than by the sound. The struggle was renewed with an agony and intenseness of energy, that betrayed itself in deep-drawn gasps. One desperate effort, which terminated in the breaking of some part of the door, producing a sound as if the door-post was wrenched from its position, was followed by another wrestle, evidently upon the narrow ledge which ran outside the door, overtopping the precipice. This seemed as fruitless as the rest, for it was followed by a crashing sound as if some heavy body had fallen over, and was rushing down the precipice, through the light boughs that crossed near the top. All then became still as the grave, except the moan of the night wind that sighed up the wooded glen.

The old servant had not nerve to return through the hall, and to him that night seemed all but endless; but morning at length came, and with it the disclosure of the events of the night. Near the door, upon the ground, lay Sir Robert's sword-belt, which had given way in the scuffle. A huge splinter from the massive door-post had been wrenched off, by an almost superhuman effort—one which nothing but the gripe of a despairing man could have severed—and on the rock outside were left the marks of the slipping and sliding of feet.

At the foot of the precipice, not immediately under the castle, but dragged some way up the glen, were found the remains of Sir Robert, with hardly a vestige of a limb or feature left distinguishable. The right hand, however was uninjured, and in its fingers was clutched, with the fixedness of death, a long lock of coarse sooty hair—the only direct circumstantial evidence of the presence of a second person. So says tradition.

This story, as I have mentioned, was current among the dealers in such lore; but the original facts are so dissimilar in all but the name of the principal person mentioned, Sir Robert Ardagh, and the fact that his death was accompanied with circumstances of extraordinary mystery, that the two narratives are totally irreconcileable, (even allowing the utmost for the exaggerating influence of tradition,) except by supposing report to have combined and blended together the fabulous histories of several distinct heroes of the family of Ardagh. However this may be, I shall lay before the reader a distinct recital of the events from which the foregoing tradition arose. With respect to these there can be no mistake; they are authenticated as fully as any thing can be by human testimony; and I state them principally upon the evidence of a lady who herself bore a prominent part in the strange events which she related, and which I now record as being among the few well-attested tales of the marvellous, which it has been my fate to hear. I shall, as far as I am able, arrange in one combined narrative, the evidence of several distinct persons, who were eye-witnesses of what they related, and with the truth of whose testimony I am solemnly and deeply impressed.

Sir Robert Ardagh was the heir and representative of the family whose name he bore; but owing to the prodigality of his father, the estates descended to him in a very impaired condition. Urged by the restless spirit of youth, or more probably by a feeling of pride, which could not submit to witness, in the paternal mansion, what he considered a humiliating alteration in the style and hospitality which up to that time had distinguished his family, Sir Robert left Ireland and went abroad. How he occupied himself, or what countries he visited during his absence, was never known, nor did he afterwards make any allusion, or encourage any inquiries touching his foreign sojourn. He left Ireland in the year 1742, being then just of age, and was not heard of until the year 1760—about eighteen years afterwards—at which time he returned. His personal appearance was, as might have been expected, very greatly altered, more altered, indeed, than the time of his absence might have warranted one in supposing likely. But to counterbalance the unfavourable change which time had wrought in his form and features, he had acquired all the advantages of polish of manner, and refinement of taste, which foreign travel is supposed to bestow. But what was truly surprising was, that it soon became evident that Sir Robert was very wealthy—wealthy to an extraordinary and unaccountable degree; and this fact was made manifest, not only by his expensive style of living, but by his proceeding to disembarrass his property, and to purchase extensive estates in addition. Moreover, there could be nothing deceptive in these appearances, for he paid ready money for every thing, from the most important purchase to the most trifling.

Sir Robert was a remarkably agreeable man, and possessing the combined advantages of birth and property, he was, as a matter of course, gladly received into the highest society which the metropolis then commanded. It was thus that he became acquainted with the two beautiful Miss F——ds, then among the brightest ornaments of the highest circles of Dublin fashion. Their family was in more than one direction allied to nobility; and Lady D——, their elder sister by many years, and some time married to a once well-known nobleman, was now their protectress. These considerations, besides the fact that the young ladies were what is usually termed heiresses, though not to a very great amount, secured to them a high position in the best society which Ireland then produced. The two young ladies differed strongly, alike in appearance and in character. The elder of the two, Emily, was generally considered the handsomer—for her beauty was of that impressive kind which never failed to strike even at the first glance, possessing all the advantages of a fine person, and of a commanding carriage. The beauty of her features strikingly assorted in character with that of her figure and deportment. Her hair was raven black and richly luxuriant, beautifully contrasting with the even, perfect whiteness of her forehead—her finely pencilled brows were black as the ringlets that clustered near them—and her eyes, full, lustrous, and animated, possessed all the power and brilliancy of the black, with more than their softness and variety of expression. She was not, however, merely the tragedy queen. When she smiled, and that was not unfrequently, the dimpling of cheek and chin, the laughing display of the small and beautiful teeth—but more than all, the roguish archness of her deep, bright eye, shewed that nature had not neglected in her the lighter and the softer characteristics of woman.

Her younger sister Mary was, as I believe not unfrequently occurs in the case of sisters, quite in the opposite style of beauty. She was light-haired, had more colour, had nearly equal grace, with much more liveliness of manner. Her eyes were of that dark grey which poets so much admire—full of expression and vivacity. She was altogether a very beautiful and animated girl—though as unlike her sister as the presence of those two qualities would permit her to be. Their dissimilarity did not stop here—it was deeper than mere appearance—the character of their minds differed almost as strikingly as did their complexion. The fair-haired beauty had a large proportion of that softness and pliability of temper which physiognomists assign as the characteristics of such complexions. She was much more the creature of impulse than of feeling, and consequently more the victim of extrinsic circumstances than was her sister. Emily, on the contrary, possessed considerable firmness and decision. She was less excitable, but when excited, her feelings were more intense and enduring. She wanted much of the gaiety, but with it the volatility of her younger sister. Her opinions were adopted, and her friendships formed more reflectively, and her affections seemed to move, as it were, more slowly, but more determinedly. This firmness of character did not amount to any thing masculine, and did not at all impair the feminine grace of her manners.

Sir Robert Ardagh was for a long time apparently equally attentive to the two sisters, and many were the conjectures and the surmises as to which would be the lady of the choice. At length, however, these doubts were determined; he proposed for and was accepted by the dark beauty, Emily T——d.

The bridals were celebrated in a manner becoming the wealth and connections of the parties; and Sir Robert and Lady Ardagh left Dublin to pass the honeymoon at the family mansion, Castle Ardagh, which had lately been fitted up in a style bordering upon magnificent. Whether in compliance with the wishes of his lady, or owing to some whim of his own, his habits were henceforward strikingly altered, and from having moved among the gayest if not the most profligate of the votaries of fashion, he suddenly settled down into a quiet, domestic, country gentleman, and seldom, if ever, visited the capital, and then his sojourns were brief as the nature of his business would permit.

Lady Ardagh, however, did not suffer from this change further than in being secluded from general society; for Sir Robert's wealth, and the hospitality which he had established in the family mansion, commanded that of such of his lady's friends and relatives as had leisure or inclination to visit the castle; and as the style of living was very handsome, and its internal resources of amusement considerable, few invitations from Sir Robert or his lady were neglected.

Many years passed quietly away, during which Sir Robert's and Lady Ardagh's hopes of issue were several times disappointed. In the lapse of all this time there occurred but one event worth recording. Sir Robert had brought with him from abroad a valet, who sometimes professed himself to be a Frenchman; at others an Italian; and at others again a German. He spoke all these languages with equal fluency, and seemed to take a kind of pleasure in puzzling the sagacity and balking the curiosity of such of the visitors at the castle as at any time happened to enter into conversation with him, or who, struck by his singularities, became inquisitive respecting his country and origin. Sir Robert called him by the French name, JACQUE; and among the lower orders he was familiarly known by the title of "Jack the devil," an appellation which originated in a supposed malignity of disposition, and a real reluctance to mix in the society of those who were believed to be his equals. This morose reserve, coupled with the mystery which enveloped all about him, rendered him an object of suspicion and inquiry to his fellow-servants, amongst whom it was whispered that this man in secret governed the actions of Sir Robert with a despotic dictation, and that as if to indemnify himself for his public and apparent servitude and self-denial, he in private exacted a degree of respectful homage from his so-called master, totally inconsistent with the relation generally supposed to exist between them.

This man's personal appearance was, to say the least of it, extremely odd; he was low in stature; and this defect was enhanced by a distortion of the spine, so considerable as almost to amount to a hunch; his features, too, had all that sharpness and sickliness of hue which generally accompany deformity; he wore his hair, which was black as soot, in heavy neglected ringlets about his shoulders, and always without powder—a peculiarity in those days. There was something unpleasant, too, in the circumstance that he never raised his eyes so as to meet those of another; this fact was often cited as a proof of his being SOMETHING NOT QUITE RIGHT, and said to result not from the timidity which is supposed in most cases

to induce this habit, but from a consciousness that his eye possessed
a power, which, if exhibited, would betray a supernatural origin.
Once, and once only, had he violated this sinister observance: it
was on the occasion of Sir Robert's hopes having been most bitterly
disappointed; his lady, after a severe and dangerous confinement,
gave birth to a dead child. Immediately after the intelligence had
been made known, a servant, having upon some business, passed
outside the gate of the castle yard, was met by Jacque, who, contrary to his wont, accosted him, observing, "so, after all the pother,
the son and heir is still-born." This remark was accompanied by a
chuckling laugh, only, the only approach to merriment which he
was ever known to exhibit. The servant, who was really disappointed, having hoped for holy-day times, feasting and debauchery
with impunity during the rejoicings which would have accompanied a christening, turned tartly upon the little valet, telling him
that he should let Sir Robert know how he had received the tidings
which should have filled any faithful servant with sorrow; and
having once broken the ice, he was proceeding with increasing
fluency, when his harangue was cut short and his temerity pun-
ished, by the little man's raising his head and treating him to a
scowl so fearful, half demoniac, half insane, that it haunted his
imagination in nightmares and nervous tremours for months after.

To this man Lady Ardagh had, at first sight, conceived an antipathy amounting to horror, a mixture of loathing and dread so
very powerful that she had made it a particular and urgent request
to Sir Robert, that he would dismiss him, offering herself, from
that property which Sir Robert had, by the marriage settlements,
left at her own disposal, to provide handsomely for him, provided
only she might be relieved from the continual anxiety and dis-
comfort which the fear of encountering him induced.

Sir Robert, however, would not hear of it; the request seemed
at first to agitate and distress him; but when still urged in defiance
of his peremptory refusal, he burst into a violent fit of fury; he
spoke darkly of great sacrifices which he had made, and threatened
that if the request were at any time renewed he would leave both
her and the country for ever. This was, however, a solitary instance
of violence; his general conduct towards Lady Ardagh, though at
no time bordering upon the uxorious, was certainly kind and
respectful, and he was more than repaid in the fervent attachment
which she bore him in return.

Some short time after this strange interview between Sir Robert
and Lady Ardagh; one night after the family had retired to bed,
and when everything had been quiet for some time, the bell of

Sir Robert's dressing-room rang suddenly and violently; the ringing was repeated again and again at still shorter intervals, and with increasing violence, as if the person who pulled the bell was agitated by the presence of some terrifying and imminent danger. A servant named Donovan was the first to answer it; he threw on his clothes, and hurried to the room with haste proportioned to the urgency of the call.

Sir Robert had selected for his private room an apartment, remote from the bed-chambers of the castle, most of which lay in the more modern parts of the mansion, and secured at its entrance by a double door; as the servant opened the first of these, Sir Robert's bell again sounded with a longer and louder peal; the inner door resisted his efforts to open it; but after a few violent struggles, not having been perfectly secured or owing to the inadequancy of the bolt itself, it gave way, and the servant rushed into the apartment, advancing several paces before he could recover himself. As he entered, he heard Sir Robert's voice exclaiming loudly "wait without, do not come in yet;" but the prohibition came too late. Near a low truckle-bed, upon which Sir Robert sometimes slept, for he was a whimsical man, in a large arm chair, sate, or rather lounged, the form of the valet, Jacque; his arms folded, and his heels stretched forward on the floor so as fully to exhibit his misshapen legs, his head thrown back, and his eyes fixed upon his master with a look of indescribable defiance and derision, while, as if to add to the strange insolence of his attitude and expression, he had placed upon his head the black cloth cap which it was his habit to wear.

Sir Robert was standing before him at the distance of several yards in a posture expressive of despair, terror, and what might be called an agony of humility. He waved his hand twice or thrice, as if to dismiss the servant, who, however, remained fixed on the spot where he had first stood; and then, as if forgetting every thing but the agony within him, he pressed his clenched hands on his cold damp brow, and dashed away the heavy drops that gathered chill and thickly there. Jacque broke the silence.

"Donovan," said he, "shake up that drone and drunkard, Carlton; tell him that his master directs that the travelling carriage shall be at the door within half an hour."

The servant paused as if in doubt as to what he should do; but his scruples were resolved by Sir Robert's saying hurriedly, "Go, go, do whatever he directs; his commands are mine, tell Carlton the same."

The servant hurried to obey, and in about half an hour the

carriage was at the door, and Jacque having directed the coachman to drive to B——n, a small town at about the distance of twelve miles, the nearest point, however, at which post horses could be obtained, stept into the vehicle which accordingly quitted the castle immediately.

Although it was a fine moonlight night, the carriage made its way but slowly, and after the lapse of two hours, the travellers had arrived at a point about eight miles from the castle, at which the road strikes through a desolate and heathy flat, sloping up, distantly at either side into bleak undulatory hills, in whose monotonous sweep the imagination beholds the heaving of some dark sluggish sea, arrested in its first commotion by some preternatural power; it is a gloomy and divested spot; there is neither tree nor habitation near it; its monotony is unbroken, except by here and there the grey front of a rock peering above the heath, and the effect is rendered yet more dreary and spectral by the exaggerated and misty shadows which the moon casts along the sloping sides of the hills. When they had gained about the centre of this tract, Carlton, the coachman, was surprised to see a figure standing, at some distance in advance, immediately beside the road, and still more so when, on coming up, he observed that it was no other than the person whom he believed to be at that moment quietly seated in the carriage; the coachman drew up, and nodding to him, the little valet exclaimed, "Carlton, I have got the start of you, the roads are heavy, so I shall even take care of myself the rest of the way; do you make your way back as best you can; and I shall follow my own nose;" so saying he chucked a purse into the lap of the coachman, and turning off at a right angle with the road he began to move rapidly away in the direction of the dark ridge, that lowered in the distance. The servant watched him until he was lost in the shadowy haze of night; and neither he nor any of the inmates of the castle saw Jacque again. His disappearance, as might have been expected, did not cause any regret among the servants and dependants at the castle; and Lady Ardagh did not attempt to conceal her delight; but with Sir Robert matters were different; for two or three days subsequent to this event, he confined himself to his room; and when he did return to his ordinary occupations, it was with a gloomy indifference which showed that he did so more from habit than from any interest he felt in them; he appeared from that moment unaccountably and strikingly changed, and thenceforward walked through life as a thing from which he could derive neither profit nor pleasure. His temper, however, so far from growing wayward or morose, became, though gloomy, very, almost unnaturally, placid and cold; but his spirits totally failed, and he became silent and abstracted.

These sombre habits of mind, as might have been anticipated, very materially affected the gay housekeeping of the castle; and the dark and melancholy spirit of its master, seemed to have communicated itself to the very domestics, almost to the very walls of the mansion. Several years rolled on in this way, and the sounds of mirth and wassail had long been strangers to the castle, when Sir Robert requested his lady, to her great astonishment, to invite some twenty or thirty of their friends to spend the Christmas, which was fast approaching, at the castle. Lady Ardagh gladly complied, and her sister Mary, who still continued unmarried, and Lady D—— were of course included in the invitations. Lady Ardagh had requested her sisters to set forward as early as possible, in order that she might enjoy a little of their society before the arrival of the other guests; and in compliance with this request they left Dublin almost immediately upon receiving the invitation, a little more than a week before the arrival of the festival which was to be the period at which the whole party were to muster.

For expedition's sake it was arranged that they should post, while Lady D—'s groom was to follow with her horses; she taking with herself her own maid and one male servant. They left the city when the day was considerably spent, and consequently made but three stages in the first day; upon the second, at about eight in the evening, they had reached the town of K——k, distant about fifteen miles from Castle Ardagh. Here owing to Miss F——d's great fatigue, she having been for a considerable time in a very delicate state of health, it was determined to put up for the night. They, accordingly, took possession of the best sitting room which the inn commanded, and Lady D—— remained in it to direct and urge the preparations for some refreshment, which the fatigues of the day had rendered necessary, while her younger sister retired to her bed-chamber to rest there for a little time, as the parlour commanded no such luxury as a sofa.

Miss F——d was, as I have already stated, at this time, in very delicate health; and upon this occasion the exhaustion of fatigue, and the dreary badness of the weather, combined to depress her spirits. Lady D—— had not been left long to herself, when the door communicating with the passage was abruptly opened, and her sister Mary entered in a state of great agitation; she sate down pale and trembling upon one of the chairs, and it was not until

a copious flood of tears had relieved her, that she became sufficiently calm to relate the cause of her excitement and distress. It
was simply this. Almost immediately upon lying down upon the
bed she sank into a feverish and unrefreshing slumber; images of
all grotesque shapes and startling colours flitted before her sleeping
fancy with all the rapidity and variety of the changes in a kaleido-
scope. At length, as she described it, a mist seemed to interpose
itself between her sight and the ever-shifting scenery which sported
before her imagination, and out of this cloudy shadow, gradually
emerged a figure whose back seemed turned towards the sleeper;
it was that of a lady, who, in perfect silence, was expressing as far
as pantomimic gesture could, by wringing her hands, and throwing
her head from side to side, in the manner of one who is exhausted
by the over indulgence, by the very sickness and impatience of
grief, the extremity of misery. For a long time she sought in vain to
catch a glimpse of the face of the apparition, who thus seemed to
stir and live before her. But at length the figure seemed to move
with an air of authority, as if about to give directions to some
inferior, and in doing so, it turned its head so as to display, with a
ghastly distinctness, the features of Lady Ardagh, pale as death,
with her dark hair all dishevelled, and her eyes dim and sunken
with weeping. The revulsion of feeling which Miss F——d experienced at this disclosure—for up to that point she had con-
templated the appearance rather with a sense of curiosity and of
interest, than of any thing deeper—was so horrible, that the shock
awoke her perfectly. She sat up in the bed, and looked fearfully
around the room, which was imperfectly lighted by a single candle
burning dimly, as if she almost expected to see the reality of her
dreadful vision lurking in some corner of the chamber. Her fears
were, however, verified, though not in the way she expected; yet
in a manner sufficiently horrible—for she had hardly time to
breathe and to collect her thoughts, when she heard, or thought
she heard, the voice of her sister, Lady Ardagh, sometimes sobbing
violently, and sometimes almost shrieking as if in terror, and calling upon her and Lady D——, with the most imploring earnest-
ness of despair, for God's sake to lose no time in coming to her.
All this was so horribly distinct, that it seemed as if the mourner
was standing within a few yards of the spot where Miss F——d lay.
She sprang from the bed, and leaving the candle in the room behind her, she made her way in the dark through the passage, the
voice still following her, until as she arrived at the door of the
sitting-room it seemed to die away in low sobbing.

As soon as Miss F——d was tolerably recovered, she declared

her determination to proceed directly, and without further loss of time to Castle Ardagh. It was not without much difficulty that Lady D—— at length prevailed upon her to consent to remain where they then were, until morning should arrive, when it was to be expected that the young lady would be much refreshed by at least remaining quiet for the night, even though sleep were out of the question. Lady D—— was convinced, from the nervous and feverish symptoms which her sister exhibited, that she had already done too much, and was more than ever satified of the necessity of prosecuting the journey no further upon that day. After some time she persuaded her sister to return to her room, where she remained with her until she had gone to bed, and appeared comparatively composed. Lady D—— then returned to the parlour, and not finding herself sleepy, she remained sitting by the fire. Her solitude was a second time broken in upon, by the entrance of her sister, who now appeared, if possible, more agitated than before. She said that Lady D—— had not long left the room, when she was roused by a repetition of the same wailing and lamentations, accompanied by the wildest and most agonized supplications that no time should be lost in coming to Castle Ardagh, and all in her sister's voice, and uttered at the same proximity as before. This time the voice had followed her to the very door of the sitting room, and until she closed it, seemed to pour forth its cries and sobs at the very threshold.

Miss F——d now most positively declared that nothing should prevent her proceeding instantly to the castle, adding that if Lady D—— would not accompany her, she would go on by herself. Superstitious feelings are at all times more or less contagious, and the last century afforded a soil much more congenial to their growth than the present. Lady D—— was so far affected by her sister's terrors, that she became, at least, uneasy; and seeing that her sister was immoveably determined upon setting forward immediately, she consented to accompany her forthwith. After a slight delay, fresh horses were procured, and the two ladies and their attendants renewed their journey, with strong injunctions to the driver to quicken their rate of travelling as much as possible, and promises of reward in case of his doing so.

Roads were then in a much worse condition throughout the south, even than they now are; and the fifteen miles which modern posting would have passed in little more than an hour and a half, were not completed even with every possible exertion in twice the time. Miss F——d had been nervously restless during the journey. Her head had been out at the carriage window every minute; and

as they approached the entrance to the castle demesne, which lay
about a mile from the building, her anxiety began to communicate
itself to her sister. The postillion had just dismounted, and was
endeavouring to open the gate—at that time a necessary trouble;
for in the middle of the last century, porter's lodges were not
common in the south of Ireland, and locks and keys almost unknown. He had just succeeded in rolling back the heavy oaken
gate, so as to admit the vehicle, when a mounted servant rode
rapidly down the avenue, and drawing up at the carriage, asked of
the postillion who the party were; and on hearing, he rode round
to the carriage window, and handed in a note which Lady D——
received. By the assistance of one of the coach-lamps they succeeded
in deciphering it. It was scrawled in great agitation, and ran thus—

My Dear Sister—my dear Sisters both,—In God's name lose no time,
I am frightened and miserable; I cannot explain all till you come. I am
too much terrified to write coherently; but understand me—hasten—do
not waste a minute. I am afraid you will come too late.   E. A.

The servant could tell nothing more than that the castle was in
great confusion, and that Lady Ardagh had been crying bitterly
all the night. Sir Robert was perfectly well. Altogether at a loss as
to the cause of Lady Ardagh's great distress, they urged their way
up the steep and broken avenue which wound through the crowd-
ing trees, whose wild and grotesque branches, now stript and naked
by the blasts of winter, stretched drearily across the road. As the
carriage drew up in the area before the door, the anxiety of the
ladies almost amounted to sickness; and scarcely waiting for the
assistance of their attendant, they sprang to the ground, and in an
instant stood at the castle door. From within were distinctly audible the sounds of lamentation and weeping, and the suppressed
hum of voices as if of those endeavouring to soothe the mourner.
The door was speedily opened, and when the ladies entered, the
first object which met their view was their sister, Lady Ardagh,
sitting on a form in the hall, weeping and wringing her hands in
deep agony. Beside her stood two old, withered crones, who were
each endeavouring in their own way to administer consolation,
without even knowing or caring what the subject of her grief
might be.

Immediately on Lady Ardagh's seeing her sisters, she started up,
fell on their necks, and kissed them again and again without
speaking, and then taking them each by a hand, still weeping
bitterly, she led them into a small room adjoining the hall, in
which burned a light, and having closed the door, she sat down

between them. After thanking them for the haste they had made, she proceeded to tell them, in words incoherent from agitation, that Sir Robert had in private, and in the most solemn manner, told her that he should die upon that night, and that he had occupied himself during the evening in giving minute directions respecting the arrangements of his funeral. Lady D—— here suggested the possibility of his labouring under the hallucinations of a fever; but to this Lady Ardagh quickly replied,

"Oh! no, no! would to God I could think it. Oh! no, no! wait till you have seen him. There is a frightful calmness about all he says and does; and his directions are all so clear, and his mind so perfectly collected, it is impossible, quite impossible;" and she wept yet more bitterly.

At that moment Sir Robert's voice was heard in issuing some directions, as he came down stairs; and Lady Ardagh exclaimed, hurriedly—

"Go now and see him yourself; he is in the hall."

Lady D—— accordingly went out into the hall, where Sir Robert met her; and saluting her with kind politeness, he said, after a pause—

"You are come upon a melancholy mission—the house is in great confusion, and some of its inmates in considerable grief." He took her hand, and looking fixedly in her face, continued— "I shall not live to see tomorrow's sun shine."

"You are ill, sir, I have no doubt," replied she; "but I am very certain we shall see you much better to-morrow, and still better the day following."

"I am *not* ill, sister," replied he: "Feel my temples, they are cool; lay your finger to my pulse, its throb is slow and temperate. I never was more perfectly in health, and yet do I know that ere three hours be past, I shall be no more."

"Sir, sir," said she, a good deal startled, but wishing to conceal the impression which the calm solemnity of his manner had, in her own despite, made upon her, "Sir, you should not jest; you should not even speak lightly upon such subjects. You trifle with what is sacred—you are sporting with the best affections of your wife——"

"Stay, my good lady," said he; "if when this clock shall strike the hour of three, I shall be anything but a helpless clod, then upbraid me. Pray return now to your sister. Lady Ardagh is, indeed, much to be pitied; but what is past cannot now be helped. I have now a few papers to arrange, and some to destroy. I shall see you and Lady Ardagh before my death; try to compose her—her sufferings distress me much; but what is past cannot now be mended."

Thus saying he went up stairs, and Lady D—— returned to the room where her sisters were sitting.

"Well," exclaimed Lady Ardagh, as she re-entered, "is it not so? —do you still doubt?—do you think there is any hope?"

Lady D—— was silent.

"Oh! none, none, none," continued she; "I see, I see you are convinced," and she wrung her hands in bitter agony.

"My dear sister," said Lady D——, "there is, no doubt, something strange in all that has appeared in this matter; but still I cannot but hope that there may be something deceptive in all the apparent calmness of Sir Robert. I still must believe that some latent fever has affected his mind, as that owing to the state of nervous depression into which he has been sinking, some trivial occurrence has been converted, in his disordered imagination, into an augury foreboding his immediate dissolution."

In such suggestions, unsatisfactory even to those who originated them, and doubly so to her whom they were intended to comfort, more than two hours passed; and Lady D—— was beginning to hope that the fated term might elapse without the occurrence of any tragical event, when Sir Robert entered the room. On coming in, he placed his finger with a warning gesture upon his lips, as if to enjoin silence; and then having successively pressed the hands of his two sisters-in-law, he stooped over the almost lifeless form of his lady, and twice pressed her cold, pale forehead with his lips, and then passed motionlessly out of the room.

Lady D—— followed to the door, saw him take a candle in the hall, and walk deliberately up the stairs. Stimulated by a feeling of horrible curiosity, she continued to follow him at a distance. She saw him enter his own private room, and heard him close and lock the door after him. Continuing to follow him as far as she could, she placed herself at the door of the chamber, as noiselessly as possible; where after a little time, she was joined by her two sisters, Lady Ardagh and Miss F——d. In breathless silence they listened to what should pass within. They distinctly heard Sir Robert pacing up and down the room for some time; and then, after a pause, a sound as if some one had thrown himself heavily upon the bed. At this moment Lady D——, forgetting that the door had been secured within, turned the handle for the purpose of entering; some one from the inside, close to the door, said, "Hush! hush!" The same lady, now much alarmed, knocked violently at the door—there was no answer. She knocked again more violently, with no further success. Lady Ardagh, now uttering a piercing shriek, sank in a swoon upon the floor. Three or four servants, alarmed by the noise, now hurried up stairs, and Lady Ardagh was carried apparently lifeless to her own chamber. They then, after having knocked long and loudly in vain, applied themselves to forcing an entrance into Sir Robert's room. After resisting some violent efforts, the door at length gave way, and all entered the room nearly together. There was a single candle burning upon a table at the far end of the apartment; and stretched upon the bed lay Sir Robert Ardagh. He was a corpse—the eyes were open—no convulsion had passed over the features, or distorted the limbs—it seemed as if the soul had sped from the body without a struggle to remain there. On touching the body it was found to be cold as clay —all lingering of the vital heat had left it. They closed the ghastly eyes of the corpse, and leaving it to the care of those who seem to consider it a privilege of their age and sex to gloat over the revolting spectacle of death in all its stages, they returned to Lady Ardagh, now a widow. The party assembled at the castle, but the atmosphere was tainted with death. Grief there was not much, but awe and panic were expressed in every face. The guests talked in whispers, and the servants walked on tiptoe, as if afraid of the very noise of their own footsteps.

The funeral was conducted almost with splendour. The body having been conveyed, in compliance with Sir Robert's last directions, to Dublin, was there laid within the ancient walls of Saint Audoen's Church—where I have read the epitaph, telling the age and titles of the departed dust. Neither painted escutcheon, nor marble slab, have served to rescue from oblivion the story of the dead, whose very name will ere long moulder from their tracery—

Et sunt sua fata sepulchris.*

The events which I have recorded are not imaginary. They are FACTS; and there lives one whose authority none would venture to question, who could vindicate the accuracy of every statement which I have set down, and that, too, with all the circumstantiality of an eye witness.†

* This prophesy has since been realised; for the aisle in which Sir Robert's remains were laid, has been suffered to fall completely to decay; and the tomb which marked his grave, and other monuments more curious, form now one indistinguishable mass of rubbish.

† This paper, from a memorandum, I find to have been written in 1803. The lady to whom allusion is made, I believe to be Miss Mary F——d. She never married, and survived both her sisters, living to a very advanced age.

Sir Dominick's Bargain

A Legend of Dunoran

In the early autumn of the year 1838, business called me to the south of Ireland. The weather was delightful, the scenery and people were new to me, and sending my luggage on by the mail-coach route in charge of a servant, I hired a serviceable nag at a posting-house, and, full of the curiosity of an explorer, I commenced a leisurely journey of five-and-twenty miles on horseback, by sequestered cross-roads, to my place of destination. By bog and hill, by plain and ruined castle, and many a winding stream, my picturesque road led me.

I had started late, and having made little more than half my journey, I was thinking of making a short halt at the next convenient place, and letting my horse have a rest and a feed, and making some provision also for the comforts of his rider.

It was about four o'clock when the road, ascending a gradual steep, found a passage through a rocky gorge between the abrupt termination of a range of mountain to my left and a rocky hill, that rose dark and sudden at my right. Below me lay a little thatched village, under a long line of gigantic beech-trees, through the boughs of which the lowly chimneys sent up their thin turf-smoke. To my left, stretched away for miles, ascending the mountain range I have mentioned, a wild park, through whose sward and ferns the rock broke, time-worn and lichen-stained. This park was studded with straggling wood, which thickened to something like a forest, behind and beyond the little village I was approaching, clothing the irregular ascent of the hillsides with beautiful, and in some places discoloured foliage.

As you descend, the road winds slightly, with the grey park-wall, built of loose stone, and mantled here and there with ivy, at its left, and crosses a shallow ford; and as I approached the village, through breaks in the woodlands, I caught glimpses of the long front of an old ruined house, placed among the trees, about half-way up the picturesque mountain-side.

The solitude and melancholy of this ruin piqued my curiosity, and when I had reached the rude thatched public-house, with the sign of St. Columbkill, with robes, mitre, and crozier, displayed over its lintel, having seen to my horse and made a good meal myself on a rasher and eggs, I began to think again of the wooded park and the ruinous house, and resolved on a ramble of half an hour among its sylvan solitudes.

The name of the place, I found, was Dunoran; and beside the gate a stile admitted to the grounds, through which, with a pensive enjoyment, I began to saunter towards the dilapidated mansion.

A long grass-grown road, with many turns and windings, led up to the old house, under the shadow of the wood.

The road, as it approached the house, skirted the edge of a precipitous glen, clothed with hazel, dwarf-oak, and thorn, and the silent house stood with its wide-open hall-door facing this dark ravine, the further edge of which was crowned with towering forest; and great trees stood about the house and its deserted court-yard and stables.

I walked in and looked about me, through passages overgrown with nettles and weeds; from room to room with ceilings rotted, and here and there a great beam dark and worn, with tendrils of ivy trailing over it. The tall walls with rotten plaster were stained and mouldy, and in some rooms the remains of decayed wain-scoting crazily swung to and fro. The almost sashless windows were darkened also with ivy, and about the tall chimneys the jackdaws were wheeling, while from the huge trees that overhung the glen in sombre masses at the other side, the rooks kept up a ceaseless cawing.

As I walked through these melancholy passages—peeping only into some of the rooms, for the flooring was quite gone in the middle, and bowed down toward the centre, and the house was very nearly un-roofed, a state of things which made the exploration a little critical—I began to wonder why so grand a house, in the midst of scenery so picturesque, had been permitted to go to decay; I dreamed of the hospitalities of which it had long ago been the rallying place, and I thought what a scene of Redgauntlet revelries it might disclose at midnight.

The great staircase was of oak, which had stood the weather wonderfully, and I sat down upon its steps, musing vaguely on the transitoriness of all things under the sun.

Except for the hoarse and distant clamour of the rooks, hardly audible where I sat, no sound broke the profound stillness of the spot. Such a sense of solitude I have seldom experienced before. The air was stirless, there was not even the rustle of a withered leaf along the passage. It was oppressive. The tall trees that stood close about the building darkened it, and added something of awe to the melancholy of the scene.

In this mood I heard, with an unpleasant surprise, close to me, a voice that was drawling, and, I fancied, sneering, repeat the words: "Food for worms, dead and rotten; God over all."

There was a small window in the wall, here very thick, which had been built up, and in the dark recess of this, deep in the shadow, I now saw a sharp-featured man, sitting with his feet dangling. His keen eyes were fixed on me, and he was smiling cynically, and before I had well recovered my surprise, he repeated the distich:

> If death was a thing that money could buy,
> The rich they would live, and the poor they would die.

"It was a grand house in its day, sir," he continued, "Dunoran House, and the Sarsfields. Sir Dominick Sarsfield was the last of the old stock. He lost his life not six foot away from where you are sitting."

As he thus spoke he let himself down, with a little jump, on to the ground.

He was a dark-faced, sharp-featured, little hunchback, and had a walking-stick in his hand, with the end of which he pointed to a rusty stain in the plaster of the wall.

"Do you mind that mark, sir?" he asked.

"Yes," I said, standing up, and looking at it, with a curious anticipation of something worth hearing.

"That's about seven or eight feet from the ground, sir, and you'll not guess what it is."

"I dare say not," said I, "unless it is a stain from the weather."

" 'Tis nothing so lucky, sir," he answered, with the same cynical smile and a wag of his head, still pointing at the mark with his stick. "That's a splash of brains and blood. It's there this hundhred years; and it will never leave it while the wall stands."

"He was murdered, then?"

"Worse than that, sir," he answered.

"He killed himself, perhaps?"

"Worse than that, itself, this cross between us and harm! I'm oulder than I look, sir; you wouldn't guess my years."

He became silent, and looked at me, evidently inviting a guess.

"Well, I should guess you to be about five-and-fifty."

He laughed, and took a pinch of snuff, and said:

"I'm that, your honour, and something to the back of it. I was seventy last Candlemas. You would not a' thought that, to look at me."

"Upon my word I should not; I can hardly believe it even now. Still, you don't remember Sir Dominick Sarsfield's death?" I said, glancing up at the ominous stain on the wall.

"No, sir, that was a long while before I was born. But my grand-father was butler here long ago, and many a time I heard tell how Sir Dominick came by his death. There was no masther in the great house ever sinst that happened. But there was two sarvants in care of it, and my aunt was one o' them; and she kep' me here wid her till I was nine year old, and she was lavin' the place to go to Dublin; and from that time it was let to go down. The wind sthript the roof, and the rain rotted the timber, and little by little, in sixty years' time, it kem to what you see. But I have a likin' for it still, for the sake of ould times; and I never come this way but I take a look in. I don't think it's many more times I'll be turnin' to see the ould place, for I'll be undher the sod myself before long."

"You'll outlive younger people," I said.

And, quitting that trite subject, I ran on:

"I don't wonder that you like this old place; it is a beautiful spot, such noble trees."

"I wish ye seen the glin when the nuts is ripe; they're the sweetest nuts in all Ireland, I think," he rejoined, with a practical sense of the picturesque. "You'd fill your pockets while you'd be lookin' about you."

"These are very fine old woods," I remarked. "I have not seen any in Ireland I thought so beautiful."

"Eiah! your honour, the woods about here is nothing to what they wor. Al the mountains along here was wood when my father was a gossoon, and Murroa Wood was the grandest of them all. All oak mostly, and all cut down as bare as the road. Not one left here that's fit to compare with them. Which way did your honour come hither—from Limerick?"

"No. Killaloe."

"Well, then, you passed the ground where Murroa Wood was in former times. You kem undher Lisnavourra, the steep knob of a hill about a mile above the village here. 'Twas near that Murroa Wood was, and 'twas there Sir Dominick Sarsfield first met the devil, the Lord between us and harm, and a bad meeting it was for him and his."

I had become interested in the adventure which had occurred in the very scenery which had so greatly attracted me, and my new acquaintance, the little hunchback, was easily entreated to tell me the story, and spoke thus, so soon as we had each resumed his seat:

"It was a fine estate when Sir Dominick came into it; and grand doings there was entirely, feasting and fiddling, free quarters for all the pipers in the counthry round, and a welcome for every one that liked to come. There was wine, by the hogshead, for the quality; and potteen enough to set a town a-fire, and beer and cidher enough to float a navy, for the boys and girls, and the likes o' me. It was kep' up the best part of a month, till the weather broke, and the rain spoilt the sod for the moneen jigs, and the fair of Allybally Killudeen comin' on they wor obliged to give over their diversion, and attind to the pigs.

But Sir Dominick was only beginnin' when they wor lavin' off. There was no way of gettin' rid of his money and estates he did not try—what with drinkin', dicin', racin', cards, and all soarts, it was not many years before the estates wor in debt, and Sir Dominick a distressed man. He showed a bold front to the world as long as he could; and then he sould off his dogs, and most of his horses, and gev out he was going to thravel in France, and the like; and so off with him for awhile; and no one in these parts heard tale or tidings of him for two or three years. Till at last quite unexpected, one night there comes a rapping at the big kitchen window. It was past ten o'clock, and old Connor Hanlon, the butler, my grandfather, was sittin' by the fire alone, warming his shins over it. There was keen east wind blowing along the mountains that night, and whistling cowld enough, through the tops of the trees, and soundin' lonesome through the long chimneys.

(And the story-teller glanced up at the nearest stack visible from his seat.)

So he wasn't quite sure of the knockin' at the window, and up he gets, and sees his master's face.

My grandfather was glad to see him safe, for it was a long time since there was any news of him; but he was sorry, too, for it was a changed place and only himself and old Juggy Broadrick in charge of the house, and a man in the stables, and it was a poor thing to see him comin' back to his own like that.

He shook Con by the hand, and says he:

"I came here to say a word to you. I left my horse with Dick in the stable; I may want him again before morning, or I may never want him."

And with that he turns into the big kitchen, and draws a stool, and sits down to take an air of the fire.

"Sit down, Connor, opposite me, and listen to what I tell you, and don't be afeard to say what you think."

He spoke all the time lookin' into the fire, with his hands stretched over it, and a tired man he looked.

"An' why should I be afeard, Masther Dominick?" says my grandfather. "Yourself was a good masther to me, and so was your father, rest his sould, before you, and I'll say the truth, and dar' the devil, and more than that, for any Sarsfield of Dunoran, much less yourself, and a good right I'd have."

"It's all over with me, Con," says Sir Dominick.

"Heaven forbid!" says my grandfather.

" 'Tis past praying for," says Sir Dominick. "The last guinea's gone; the ould place will follow it. It must be sold, and I'm come here, I don't know why, like a ghost to have a last look round me, and go off in the dark again."

And with that he tould him to be sure, in case he should hear of his death, to give the oak box, in the closet off his room, to his cousin, Pat Sarsfield, in Dublin, and the sword and pistols his grandfather carried in Aughrim, and two or three thrifling things of the kind.

And says he, "Con, they say if the divil gives you money over-night, you'll find nothing but a bagful of pebbles, and chips, and nutshells, in the morning. If I thought he played fair, I'm in the humour to make a bargain with him to-night."

"Lord forbid!" says my grandfather, standing up, with a start, and crossing himself.

"They say the country's full of men, listin' sogers for the King o' France. If I light on one o' them, I'll not refuse his offer. How contrary things goes! How long is it since me an Captain Waller fought the jewel at New Castle?"

"Six years, Masther Dominick, and ye broke his thigh with the bullet the first shot."

"I did, Con," says he, "and I wish, instead, he had shot me through the heart. Have you any whisky?"

My grandfather took it out of the buffet, and the masther pours out some into a bowl, and drank it off.

"I'll go out and have a look at my horse," says he, standing up. There was sort of a stare in his eyes, as he pulled his riding-cloak about him, as if there was something bad in his thoughts.

"Sure, I won't be a minute running out myself to the stable, and looking after the horse for you myself," says my grandfather.

"I'm not goin' to the stable," says Sir Dominick; "I may as well tell you, for I see you found it out already—I'm goin' across the deer-park; if I come back you'll see me in an hour's time. But, anyhow, you'd better not follow me, for if you do I'll shoot you, and that 'id be a bad ending to our friendship."

And with that he walks down this passage here, and turns the key in the side door at that end of it, and out wid him on the sod into the moonlight and the cowld wind; and my grandfather seen him walkin' hard towards the park-wall, and then he comes in and closes the door with a heavy heart.

Sir Dominick stopped to think when he got to the middle of the deer-park, for he had not made up his mind, when he left the house, and the whisky did not clear his head, only it gev him courage.

He did not feel the cowld wind now, nor fear death, nor think much of anything but the shame and fall of the old family.

And he made up his mind, if no better thought came to him between that and there, so soon as he came to Murroa Wood, he'd hang himself from one of the oak branches with his cravat.

It was a bright moonlight night, there was just a bit of a cloud driving across the moon now and then, but, only for that, as light a'most as day.

Down he goes, right for the wood of Murroa. It seemed to him every step he took was as long as three, and it was no time till he was among the big oak-trees with their roots spreading from one to another, and their branches stretching overhead like the timbers of a naked roof, and the moon shining down through them, and casting their shadows thick and twist abroad on the ground as black as my shoe.

He was sobering a bit by this time, and he slacked his pace, and he thought 'twould be better to list in the French king's army, and thry what that might do for him, for he knew a man might take his own life any time, but it would puzzle him to take it back again when he liked.

Just as he made up his mind not to make away with himself, what should he hear but a step clinkin' along the dry ground under the trees, and soon he sees a grand gentleman right before him comin' up to meet him.

He was a handsome young man like himself, and he wore a cocked-hat with gold-lace round it, such as officers wears on their coats, and he had on a dress the same as French officers wore in them times.

He stopped opposite Sir Dominick, and he cum to a standstill also.

The two gentlemen took off their hats to one another, and says the stranger:

"I am recruiting, sir," says he, "for my sovereign, and you'll find my money won't turn into pebbles, chips, and nutshells, by to-morrow."

At the same time he pulls out a big purse full of gold.

The minute he set eyes on that gentleman, Sir Dominick had his own opinion of him; and at those words he felt the very hair standing up on his head.

"Don't be afraid," says he, "the money won't burn you. If it proves honest gold, and if it prospers with you, I'm willing to make a bargain. This is the last day of February," says he; "I'll serve you seven years, and at the end of that time you shall serve me, and I'll come for you when the seven years is over, when the clock turns the minute between February and March; and the first of March ye'll come away with me, or never. You'll not find me a bad master, any more than a bad servant. I love my own; and I command all the pleasures and the glory of the world. The bargain dates from this day, and the lease is out at midnight on the last day I told you; and in the year"—he told him the year, it was easy reckoned, but I forget it—"and if you'd rather wait," he says, "for eight months and twenty eight days, before you sign the writin', you may, if you meet me here. But I can't do a great deal for you in the mean time; and if you don't sign then, all you get from me, up to that time, will vanish away, and you'll be just as you are to-night, and ready to hang yourself on the first tree you meet."

Well, the end of it was, Sir Dominick chose to wait, and he came back to the house with a big bag full of money, as round as your hat a'most.

My grandfather was glad enough, you may be sure, to see the master safe and sound again so soon. Into the kitchen he bangs again, and swings the bag o' money on the table; and he stands up straight, and heaves up his shoulders like a man that has just got shut of a load; and he looks at the bag, and my grandfather looks at him, and from him to it, and back again. Sir Dominick looked as white as a sheet, and says he:

"I don't know, Con, what's in it; it's the heaviest load I ever carried."

He seemed shy of openin' the bag; and he made my grandfather heap up a roaring fire of turf and wood, and then, at last, he opens it, and, sure enough, 'twas stuffed full o' golden guineas, bright and new, as if they were only that minute out o' the Mint.

Sir Dominick made my grandfather sit at his elbow while he counted every guinea in the bag.

When he was done countin', and it wasn't far from daylight when that time came, Sir Dominick made my grandfather swear not to tell a word about it. And a close secret it was for many a day after.

When the eight months and twenty-eight days were pretty near spent and ended, Sir Dominick returned to the house here with a troubled mind, in doubt what was best to be done, and no one alive but my grandfather knew anything about the matter, and he not half what had happened.

As the day drew near, towards the end of October, Sir Dominick grew only more and more troubled in mind.

One time he made up his mind to have no more to say to such things, nor to speak again with the like of them he met with in the wood of Murroa. Then, again, his heart failed him when he thought of his debts, and he not knowing where to turn. Then, only a week before the day, everything began to go wrong with him. One man wrote from London to say that Sir Dominick paid three thousand pounds to the wrong man, and must pay it over again; another demanded a debt he never heard of before; and another, in Dublin, denied the payment of a thundherin' big bill, and Sir Dominick could nowhere find the receipt, and so on, wid fifty other things as bad.

Well, by the time the night of the 28th of October came round, he was a'most ready to lose his senses with all the demands that was risin' up again him on all sides, and nothing to meet them but the help of the one dhreadful friend he had to depind on at night in the oak-wood down there below.

So there was nothing for it but to go through with the business that was begun already, and about the same hour as he went last, he takes off the little crucifix he wore round his neck, for he was a Catholic, and his gospel, and his bit o' the thrue cross that he had in a locket, for since he took the money from the Evil One he was growin' frightful in himself, and got all he could to guard him from the power of the devil. But to-night, for his life, he daren't take them with him. So he gives them into my grandfather's hands without a word, only he looked as white as a sheet o' paper; and he takes his hat and sword, and telling my grandfather to watch for him, away he goes, to try what would come of it.

It was a fine still night, and the moon—not so bright, though, now as the first time—was shinin' over heath and rock, and down on the lonesome oak-wood below him.

His heart beat thick as he drew near it. There was not a sound, not even the distant bark of a dog from the village behind him. There was not a lonesomer spot in the country round, and if it wasn't for his debts and losses that was drivin' him on half mad, in spite of his fears for his soul and his hopes of paradise, and all his good angel was whisperin' in his ear, he would a' turned back, and sent for his clargy, and made his confession and his penance, and changed his ways, and led a good life, for he was frightened enough to have done a great dale.

Softer and slower he stept as he got, once more, in undher the big branches of the oak-threes; and when he got in a bit, near where he met with the bad spirit before, he stopped and looked round him, and felt himself, every bit, turning as cowld as a dead man, and you may be sure he did not feel much betther when he seen the same man steppin' from behind the big tree that was touchin' his elbow a'most.

"You found the money good," says he, "but it was not enough. No matter, you shall have enough and to spare. I'll see after your luck, and I'll give you a hint whenever it can serve you; and any time you want to see me you have only to come down here, and call my face to mind, and wish me present. You shan't owe a shilling by the end of the year, and you shall never miss the right card, the best throw, and the winning horse. Are you willing?"

The young gentleman's voice almost stuck in his throat, and his hair was rising on his head, but he did get out a word or two to signify that he consented; and with that the Evil One handed him a needle, and bid him give him three drops of blood from his arm; and he took them in the cup of an acorn, and gave him a pen, and bid him write some words that he repeated, and that Sir Dominick did not understand, on two thin slips of parchment. He took one himself and the other he sunk in Sir Dominick's arm at the place where he drew the blood, and he closed the flesh over it. And that's as true as you're sittin' there!

Well, Sir Dominick went home. He was a frightened man, and well he might be. But in a little time he began to grow aisier in his mind. Anyhow, he got out of debt very quick, and money came tumbling in to make him richer, and everything he took in hand prospered, and he never made a wager, or played a game, but he won; and for all that, there was not a poor man on the estate that was not happier than Sir Dominick.

So he took again to his old ways; for, when the money came back, all came back, and there were hounds and horses, and wine galore, and no end of company, and grand doin's, and divarsion, up here at the great house. And some said Sir Dominick was thinkin' of gettin' married; and more said he wasn't. But, anyhow, there was somethin' troublin' him more than common, and so one night, unknownst to all, away he goes to the lonesome oak-wood. It was something, maybe, my grandfather thought was troublin' him about a beautiful young lady he was jealous of, and mad in love with her. But that was only guess.

Well, when Sir Dominick got into the wood this time, he grew more in dread than ever; and he was on the point of turnin' and lavin' the place, when who should he see, close beside him, but my gentleman, seated on a big stone undher one of the trees. In place of looking the fine young gentleman in goold lace and grand clothes he appeared before, he was now in rags, he looked twice the size he had been, and his face smutted with soot, and he had a murtherin' big steel hammer, as heavy as a half-hundred, with a handle a yard long, across his knees. It was so dark under the tree, he did not see him quite clear for some time.

He stood up, and he looked awful tall entirely. And what passed between them in that discourse my grandfather never heered. But Sir Dominick was as black as night afterwards, and hadn't a laugh for anything nor a word a'most for any one, and he only grew worse and worse, and darker and darker. And now this thing, whatever it was, used to come to him of its own accord, whether he wanted it or no; sometimes in one shape, and sometimes in another, in lonesome places, and sometimes at his side by night when he'd be ridin' home alone, until at last he lost heart altogether and sent for the priest.

The priest was with him a long time, and when he heered the whole story, he rode off all the way for the bishop, and the bishop came here to the great house next day, and he gev Sir Dominick a good advice. He toult him he must give over dicin', and swearin,' and drinkin', and all bad company, and live a vartuous steady life until the seven years' bargain was out, and if the divil didn't come for him the minute afther the stroke of twelve the first morning of the month of March, he was safe out of the bargain. There was not more than eight or ten months to run now before the seven years wor out, and he lived all the time according to the bishop's advice, as strict as if he was "in retreat."

Well, you may guess he felt quare enough when the mornin' of the 28th of February came.

The priest came up by appointment, and Sir Dominick and his raverence wor together in the room you see there, and kep' up their prayers together till the clock struck twelve, and a good hour after, and not a sign of a disturbance, nor nothing came near them, and the priest slep' that night in the house in the room next Sir Dominick's, and all went over as comfortable as could be, and they shook hands and kissed like two comrades after winning a battle.

So, now, Sir Dominick thought he might as well have a pleasant evening, after all his fastin' and praying; and he sent round to half a dozen of the neighbouring gentlemen to come and dine with him, and his raverence stayed and dined also, and a roarin' bowl o' punch they had, and no end o' wine, and the swearin' and dice, and cards and guineas changing hands, and songs and stories, that wouldn't do any one good to hear, and the priest slipped away, when he seen the turn things was takin', and it was not far from the stroke of twelve when Sir Dominick, sitting at the head of his table, swears, "this is the best first of March I ever sat down with my friends."

"It ain't the first o' March," says Mr. Hiffernan of Ballyvoreen. He was a scholard, and always kep' an almanack.

"What is it, then?" says Sir Dominick, startin' up, and dhroppin' the ladle into the bowl, and starin' at him as if he had two heads.

" 'Tis the twenty-ninth of February, leap year," says he. And just as they were talkin', the clock strikes twelve; and my grandfather, who was half asleep in a chair by the fire in the hall, openin' his eyes, sees a short square fellow with a cloak on, and long black hair bushin' out from under his hat, standin' just there where you see the bit o' light shinin' again' the wall.

(My hunchbacked friend pointed with his stick to a little patch of red sunset light that relieved the deepening shadow of the passage.)

"Tell your master," says he, in an awful voice, like the growl of a baist, "that I'm here by appointment, and expect him down-stairs this minute."

Up goes my grandfather, by these very steps you are sittin' on.

"Tell him I can't come down yet," says Sir Dominick, and he turns to the company in the room; and says he with a cold sweat shinin' on his face, "for God's sake, gentlemen, will any of you

TRINIDAD HIGH SCHOOL
LIBRARY

jump from the window and bring the priest here?" One looked at another and no one knew what to make of it, and in the mean time, up comes my grandfather again, and says he, tremblin', "He says, sir, unless you go down to him, he'll come up to you."

"I don't understand this, gentlemen, I'll see what it means," says Sir Dominick, trying to put a face on it, and walkin' out o' the room like a man through the press-room, with the hangman waitin' for him outside. Down the stairs he comes, and two or three of the gentlemen peeping over the banisters, to see. My grandfather was walking six or eight steps behind him, and he seen the stranger take a stride out to meet Sir Dominick, and catch him up in his arms, and whirl his head against the wall, and wi' that the hall-doore flies open, and out goes the candles, and the turf and wood-ashes flyin' with the wind out o' the hall-fire, ran in a drift o' sparks along the floore by his feet.

Downs runs the gintlemen. Bang goes the hall-doore. Some comes runnin' up, and more runnin' down, with lights. It was all over with Sir Dominick. They lifted up the corpse, and put its shoulders again' the wall; but there was not a gasp left in him. He was cowld and stiffenin' already.

Pat Donovan was comin' up to the great house late that night and after he passed the little brook, that the carriage track up to the house crosses, and about fifty steps to this side of it, his dog, that was by his side, makes a sudden wheel, and springs over the wall, and sets up a yowlin' inside you'd hear a mile away; and that minute two men passed him by in silence, goin' down from the house, one of them short and square, and the other like Sir Dominick in shape, but there was little light under the trees where he was, and they looked only like shadows; and as they passed him by he could not hear the sound of their feet and he drew back to the wall frightened; and when he got up to the great house, he found all in confusion, and the master's body, with the head smashed to pieces, lying just on *that spot*.

The narrator stood up and indicated with the point of his stick the exact site of the body, and, as I looked, the shadow deepened, the red stain of sunlight vanished from the wall, and the sun had gone down behind the distant hill of New Castle, leaving the haunted scene in the deep grey of darkening twilight.

So I and the story-teller parted, not without good wishes on both sides, and a little "tip," which seemed not unwelcome, from me.

It was dusk and the moon up by the time I reached the village, remounted my nag, and looked my last on the scene of the terrible legend of Dunoran.